KT-448-867

WHAT Holly DID

JOAN LINGARD

READING BOROUGH COUNCIL	
3412600336924	
PETERS	21-Aug-2012
CFTR	

CATNIP BOOKS
Published by Catnip Publishing Ltd
14 Greville Street
London EC1N 8SB

This edition first published 2012
1 3 5 7 9 10 8 6 4 2

Text copyright © Joan Lingard, 2012

The moral right of the author has been asserted

All rights reserved. No part of this publication may be reproduced, stored
in a retrieval system, or transmitted in any form or by any means electronic,
mechanical, photocopying, recording or otherwise, without prior permission
of the copyright owner.

A CIP catalogue record for this book is available from the British Library

ISBN 978-1-84647-156-8

Printed in Poland

www.catnippublishing.co.uk

One

'Are you there, Holly?' called Dad. He was in the hall, hovering outside her door.

'Of course you're here,' said Sylvie. 'Where else would you be?'

'Coming,' Holly called, ignoring Sylvie, which was easy since she wasn't there – not really. Holly sprang up from the floor where she'd been sprawled, reading, retied her ponytail and went through to the living room where her father was now sitting very upright in an armchair. He must have something on his mind.

'Come and sit down, love,' Dad said.

She took the chair opposite him, at the other side of the unlit gas fire. She felt wary. What did he want?

'Who was that you were talking to just now?' he asked quietly.

So that was it. Had he been listening at her door? Maybe she should have lied but instead Holly shrugged.

Dad said nothing, just looked at her, so he knew perfectly well.

'He doesn't like you talking to me,' said Sylvie.

Usually Holly remembered not to talk out loud to Sylvie but sometimes she forgot. Their conversations were private, and they usually took place inside her head. But she'd been reading Sylvie a passage from h' book. That must have been what Dad had heard. Well, better to talk to Sylvie than to herself, surely. Both Mum and Dad dismissed Sylvie as Holly's imaginary friend, but she was more than that. She'd been with Holly for a long time. And she was all the more important to her now Holly had come to live with Dad in Edinburgh.

There was an awkward silence. One of many. It was as if Dad didn't quite know how to talk to her, and to be honest, Holly wasn't quite sure how to talk to him. They were still getting to know each other.

'You can talk to me . . .' He watched her nervously.

Holly had an idea. 'Oh, I know . . . I talked to Johnny earlier,' she said. 'You must have heard me on the phone.'

Johnny Nightingale was her best friend. His mother Nina had rescued Holly earlier that year when she'd been stranded in Waverley Station in Edinburgh. There had been a mix-up in the arrangements between her mum and dad and she might have been stranded on her own for two whole weeks if Nina hadn't taken her home.

'I'm going to see him tomorrow, for Sunday lunch,' added Holly. Now that it was the summer holiday, and Dad was out at work all day, the arrangement was that she could go to the Nightingales' as often as she wanted. She loved it there, where it was almost as if she was part of the family. She usually spent Sunday with Mum, but she was in Tenerife on holiday at the moment. It had been one of her sudden decisions. Holly wasn't sure when her Mum would be back home.

Dad frowned. 'That's awkward.'

'Why?'

'That's what I was wanting to talk to you about.'

So it wasn't Sylvie that was bothering him. Holly sat forward in her chair. Dad looked serious. Maybe he was thinking of going back to work on the oil rigs out in the Middle East. He'd earned much more money doing that than he did in his present job. He'd only started working in Edinburgh so that he could look after her, so if he went back to the Middle East she might have to go back to live with Mum in Glasgow. But the Social Services would never agree to that, surely?

Holly couldn't decide how she felt about the way things had worked out. She knew she was better looked after by Dad, but she couldn't help missing her old life in Glasgow. Mum was a bit scatty, certainly, but she wasn't *bad*. Part of the problem was that she worked in a nightclub called the *Silver Spike* and often didn't get home until two or three in the morning, which meant that Holly was left on her own in the flat. Holly didn't usually mind, well, not too much. She'd always had Sylvie to talk to and keep her company.

But the other problem was Lenny. Or Lenny the Lion, as he once said Holly could call him. Lenny the Louse, more like, but Holly had tried to stop thinking of him like that as Lenny didn't take a teasing. He was Mum's boyfriend. The people at the Social Services did not approve of him at all and neither did Dad.

Dad took a deep breath. 'I wanted to take you to Portobello tomorrow,' he said. 'At the seaside.'

Holly knew very well that Portobello was by the sea. But what was so special about going there tomorrow?

He was always going on about it, telling her what a nice part of town it was, saying they'd sell this flat and buy a bungalow there, if they could afford it. At present they were living in a top floor flat, three storeys up, on a long, busy, city centre street. Holly quite liked it. There was always lots going on.

Her dad cleared his throat. 'A friend has invited us to lunch,' he said, not looking her straight in the eye.

'I bet it's a woman,' said Sylvie, quick as a flash.

'But Dad,' Holly protested, trying to ignore Sylvie's comment, 'Nina has already invited me to lunch. I've accepted.'

'You could see them another day, couldn't you? You'll be going on Monday, anyway, now that Johnny's on holiday too. You've the whole summer holiday to see them.' He stood up and walked over to the window. There was another awkward silence. Finally Dad swivelled round to face Holly. 'I'm sure Nina wouldn't mind if you called off.'

Nina might not mind, but Holly would. 'But I promised, Dad –' She couldn't hide her disappointment. And who was this *friend* in Portobello anyway?

'Holly, I want you to come. I can explain to Nina –'
'Dad –'

'He's not going to give in,' chanted Sylvie. 'You can tell. It must be serious.'

Sylvie could be annoying, but she was often right. Holly fell back in her chair, folded her arms across her chest and scowled. Now she thought of it, her dad had been quite secretive of late, sometimes coming home a bit later than usual and being vague about where he'd been.

Dad had another go at clearing his throat. 'This is quite a special friend, you see, love. Cerise and I actually went to the same school.' He gave a little laugh. What was so funny about that?

'Cerise! What sort of a name is *that*?!' Sylvie had strong opinions about many things.

'Cerise? I've never heard that name before.' It was the only thing Holly could think of to say.

Her dad was getting flustered. 'Well, as a matter of fact, she wasn't called Cerise when we were at school. She changed her name when she was older.'

'From what?'

'Beryl.'

Sylvie snorted.

'Why did she change her name from Beryl?' Holly couldn't help asking.

'It doesn't matter, does it, what her name was?' Dad was getting shirty. 'She's called Cerise now and that's all you need to know. I like her. And she happens to be on her own too. With a daughter,' he added hastily.

On her own too. Holly wanted to point out that he wasn't on his own if he had Holly, but decided against it.

'What's she called? The daughter?' she asked, knowing she sounded a bit rude.

'Almondine.'

'*What*?'

'Almond – like the nut – you add on the "ine". So it makes Almondine. It's maybe French.'

'Only a nut would think of that,' observed Sylvie. Holly

dipped her head so that Dad wouldn't see her smiling.

'She's just a bit older than you,' Dad went on. 'Thirteen, I think. Nice girl. I'm sure you'll get on well together.'

Dad must have been planning this for a while. He seemed to have everything sorted out.

'She's dying to meet you.' His voice was gentler now.

'Who? Almondine?'

'Cerise. Almondine, too, of course. Both of them.'

Holly fell silent. Suddenly she missed her mother badly and wished she hadn't gone off with Lenny on holiday. She had been thinking about her that morning, imagining her lying in the sun and getting a lovely golden tan. Her mum loved the sun and Lenny seemed to earn enough money, one way and another, for trips abroad. Dad occasionally muttered about how exactly Lenny earned the money. He had a few dodgy friends, which was why Holly wasn't allowed to go to Mum's flat in Glasgow any more. Her mum always came through to Edinburgh to see her on a Sunday and Dad would *never* have made her cancel an arrangement with Mum.

'She's a hairdresser,' he said, turning back to straighten the curtains.

'Who?'

'Cerise, of course,' he said. He was clearly on edge. 'She's got her own salon.'

'That's nice.'

'She could do your hair for you.'

'I don't want my hair done.' Holly flicked her ponytail over her shoulder the way her mum did.

Dad picked up an empty mug and took it through

to the kitchen. She heard him rinsing it out, then he marched back through to the living room.

'Holly,' he said firmly, 'I want you to come with me tomorrow. I think you'll enjoy yourself. Would you like me to phone Nina and explain?'

'No, it's all right, I'll do it.' Holly tried to keep the sigh from her voice. She hated letting Nina down, but it was obvious this was important to her father.

She went through to her room, closed the door and flung herself down on the bed. She lay looking at the ceiling for a few moments, then reached for her mobile.

Nina wasn't in the least put out with Holly cancelling tomorrow's lunch. She always looked on the bright side. 'Holly, you should be pleased that your dad's got a friend. It's lonely for a man bringing up a young girl on his own. Lonely for anyone.'

Holly had nothing to say in answer to that. Neither did Sylvie, for once.

'Come over on Monday, as we arranged with your dad.' There was a bus that went from the end of Holly's road to Nina's, which Holly was allowed to take on her own. 'You can tell me then how you got on.'

Two

The next day turned out to be wet.

'Just our luck,' Holly's dad groused, pulling up his hood. 'And the car's miles away. There were no spaces last night.'

Rain was coming down like stair rods, to use one of Holly's mum's sayings. Holly had put on her smartest jacket, but it didn't have a hood and her hair looked like rats' tails by the time they reached the car. Theirs was a long street. A mile or so.

'You should have put on your anorak,' Dad called out as they ran.

'Yuck,' said Holly, but he didn't hear for the sound of the rain. She hated wearing an anorak, though she had to admit that it might have been a good idea today. Her jacket was soaked, as were her new patent leather shoes.

'Maybe we should go back, Dad. I'm wringing wet.'

'Your own fault. Get in the car. We're going to be late as it is.'

That was because Holly had spent ages doing her hair. Mum had given her new straighteners and she was still getting used to them. All that effort and now look at it!

In the car Dad said, 'Cerise'll give you a towel to dry your hair off and I expect Almondine can lend you something to put on.'

Holly scowled but Dad was too busy clearing the steamed-up windows to notice. She didn't want Cerise's towel and as for putting on Almondine's clothes! What was he thinking?

They didn't speak all the way to Portobello. Holly was in no mood to utter even a word and her dad was too busy peering through the windscreen. The wipers were zigzagging furiously in their fight against the rain. At one point they almost gave up. Holly wished her dad would give up so they could go home. She had a bad feeling in the pit of her stomach.

'Nothing's going too well so far,' commented Sylvie.

Maybe that was an omen.

When they pulled up in front of Cerise's bungalow Dad switched off the engine and said with a sigh, 'Doesn't look like the sun's going to come out. I was hoping you would be able to go for a walk with Almondine along the promenade.'

'And leave him alone with Cerise,' said Sylvie.

He turned to look Holly in the eye. 'Come on then, love. And make an effort for my sake, OK?'

'OK,' muttered Holly. She gave him a quick smile and he smiled back. He looked excited all of a sudden.

'Right. Ready steady . . . go!'

They ducked their heads and dashed up the path.

Cerise must have been watching for them. She had already opened the door into the porch.

'You're soaking wet!' she exclaimed, as if deeply shocked. What else did she expect them to be on a day like this? 'Just a tick and I'll put some paper down.' Off she trotted in her strappy sandals leaving the pair of them standing, dripping onto the mat.

She was back in a flash, laying a path of newspaper all the way down the hall. It was only when she had reached the porch that Holly and her dad were permitted to enter.

'Did you not even have an umbrella?' she asked.

'We should have brought one . . .' Holly's dad was apologetic.

'You never use one, Dad,' said Holly.

'I'm not a great fan.' he admitted, giving her a look.

'Black mark for that,' sang Sylvie.

'Sorry if we're messing up your floor, Cerise,' Dad said.

'Don't worry, Joe.' Cerise leant over and kissed him, leaving the bright pink imprint of her lips on his cheek. Holly was surprised to see that there was any lipstick left on her lips! 'It's lovely to see you. Best come into the kitchen and we'll see if we can dry the two of you off.' She beckoned them along the newspaper path, running ahead to spread more sheets of newspaper on the kitchen floor. Soon they were standing there, each on their own little island.

Cerise watched, hands on hips, while they stripped off their sodden jackets. 'Best leave your shoes here to dry.'

As instructed, Holly and her dad stepped out of their shoes, leaving them on the newspapers. They were now in their stockinged feet. Holly noticed that her pale blue socks, which she'd worn yesterday as well, were none too clean. But worse was to come.

'Your hair's needing a good rub,' said Cerise. 'It's dripping wet.'

She then attacked Holly's hair, towelling it so vigorously that Holly thought she might have no scalp left at the end of it all. She emerged from under the towel blinking. Her carefully straightened hair must now be all over the place and in a pretty awful mess.

There was no sign yet of Almondine.

'Something to be grateful for at least,' said Sylvie. 'She might have gone out in the rain and got washed all the way out to sea.'

By now Cerise had started on Holly's dad's hair even though he was protesting that it was fine, it would dry by itself.

'You need looking after, Joe.' Cerise's voice had turned all soppy and affectionate.

'That woman will eat him up,' commented Sylvie. 'Chomp, chomp.'

Now that Holly had a moment's peace, she took a good look at Cerise as she fussed around Holly's dad. She would have been tall even without the sandals, and she was what Mum would call 'well built'. Her carefully styled golden hair gleamed under the kitchen light. There was not a strand out of place. It was as if it had been glued into position. Holly looked outside at the perfectly manicured garden. The world looked grey and, of course, wet. Even so, Holly would have willingly run straight out into it.

Cerise threw the towels into her washing machine, and turned to look Holly over. 'What age did you say she was, Joe?' It was as if Holly couldn't speak for herself.

'Holly's eleven.' Dad looked slightly uncomfortable.

'My goodness! Not exactly tall for your age, are you?' Cerise sounded doubtful. Then she smiled, a rather pitying smile. 'Never mind, Holly, some people shoot up like beanstalks later.'

'Perhaps Holly would like to tidy herself up in the bathroom?' suggested her dad. He knew how she felt when people commented on her height. The growth spurt Mum had always promised was a long time coming. Besides, what was so wrong with being short? 'Have you got a comb with you, love?'

Of course she did. Mum had taught her always to take a comb with her.

'First door on the left,' chirruped Cerise, pointing down the hall. 'You'll find a guest towel on the top rail.'

'Better be careful to use the right one,' Sylvie mimicked Cerise's sing-song voice.

Holly was about to make a move when the kitchen door opened and Almondine walked in. It couldn't have been anybody else. She was a smaller, younger version of her mother – much taller than Holly, though. She too had smooth golden hair and she wore four-inch heels, along with a very short pink skirt and a white top that was sliding off her shoulders.

'Almondine,' said her mother, tipping her head to one side, 'come and meet Holly.'

The girl glanced briefly at Holly, taking in her messy hair and damp trousers. 'Hi,' she said in a languid, bored voice. 'Mum, when's lunch? I'm starving.'

'We'll be eating straightaway.' Cerise began shuffling round plates near the cooker. 'Wash your hands, now.'

'Can Marnie stay for lunch?'

Only then did Holly notice that there was a girl standing in the doorway behind Almondine. They were about the same height, the two of them, and they wore the same kind of clothes and shoes. They could have been twins if Marnie's hair had not been brown.

Cerise opened and closed the oven door with more force than Holly felt was necessary. 'Oh, all right,' she agreed. A bit snappily, Holly thought. 'You'll need to set another place, dear.'

Holly was seated at the table between Almondine and her dad. Almondine and Marnie whispered and giggled together throughout the meal. From time to time Cerise ticked them off, saying, 'Manners, girls!' They paid no attention.

'They're awful,' pronounced Sylvie unnecessarily.

The meal was awful, too in Holly's opinion. Shop bought burgers that looked and tasted like the sole of your shoe. (Holly's dad made his own burgers from the local butcher's mince. His cooking was one of the pleasant surprises she'd had when she came to live with him.) Holly would normally have enjoyed chips – especially the ones from the chip shop across the road from the flat – but these were burnt. They snapped between your teeth. It was probably their fault, her and her dad's, for arriving late and coming in so wet they had to be dried off. For seconds, Cerise gave them pink-and-white ice cream, which was fine, except that they each got only a thin slice.

'She's not much of a cook then,' commented Sylvie.

The thought cheered Holly. Her dad liked nice food.

'Delicious, Cerise,' he declared, as he laid his ice cream spoon to rest.

'What a cod!' said Sylvie, sharing Holly's outrage.

'Glad you enjoyed it, Joe,' said Cerise.

They exchanged gooey smiles.

Sylvie groaned. 'This isn't looking good.' Holly wished she would be quiet. It was bad enough watching them without Sylvie's running commentary.

As soon as they'd finished eating, Almondine and Marnie pushed their chairs back from the table.

'And where do you think you two are going?' demanded Cerise, gathering the plates.

'Upstairs.'

'Well, you can take Holly with you. Joe and I will take our coffees into the living room.'

Holly saw Almondine and Marnie roll their eyes at each other and she started to protest – she didn't want to go off with the girls – but Dad cut her off, saying, 'On you go, Holly. Go and get to know your new friends!'

Three

Holly followed the girls up the narrow, steep stairs, her eyes on their wobbling heels. Perhaps Almondine would trip and sprain her ankle – or maybe both ankles. She and Marnie were whispering together and for a moment, when they dissolved into yet another fit of giggles about something or other, it looked as if Almondine might do just that, then she clutched the banister and steadied herself. Pity.

'Not very nice of you,' chided Sylvie.

Holly didn't feel like being nice, especially to those two.

Almondine's bedroom was in the attic. The colours shrieked at you as soon as you opened the door: cherry red, orange, eggy yellow, livid lime. Holly blinked. Her bedroom at Dad's might not be the most beautiful in the world, but at least it didn't give her a headache.

The two friends collapsed straightaway in a heap on top of the bed, enjoying their private joke. Holly thought of turning tail and heading back downstairs but she wouldn't be wanted there any more than she was here. Dad had made that quite clear. The rain was still drumming on the roof, so a walk along the promenade wasn't an option either. There was no escape.

Holly stood awkwardly in the doorway until she

noticed an orange chair at the back of the room. She picked her way over piles of discarded clothes and magazines and went and perched on the edge of it. The two girls were still giggling and whispering together. Holly shifted uncomfortably, looking for something to do. They were talking about her, she knew that. Every now and then they'd look at her, shield their mouths with their hands and babble into the other's ear. That was the signal for them to fold up again and start shrieking.

After a few minutes they didn't even try to keep their voices low. They were talking about Holly's clothes. *Who wore black trousers these days? Did she find that T-shirt in a charity shop? Only old grannies wear cardigans.* They went on and on. And now her hair. *What a sight!*

Holly's cheeks burned as one insult followed another.

'How long are you going to put up with this?' asked Sylvie.

Holly took a deep breath and jumped to her feet.

'Excuse me,' she said in what she hoped was a firm voice.

The girls lay on their backs staring up at her, surprised by her sudden movement. Holly went and stood over them, her hands on her hips.

'I've never come across anyone as rude and stupid as the two of you. And you're dead boring with it. Why don't you get a life?' It wasn't particularly clever, but that didn't bother Holly. She'd stick to saying what she meant. So with that she turned, walked out of the room and stamped down the stairs.

'Marvellous!' applauded Sylvie.

But now that she'd had her outburst, Holly wasn't so sure. When she opened the sitting room door, her dad and Cerise were sitting close on the settee. Cerise's long pink fingernails were curled round Dad's broad hand.

At Holly's abrupt entrance they stopped talking, dropped hands and sat up straight.

Dad cleared his throat and smiled at her, embarrassed. 'What are you doing down here, love?' he asked. 'I thought you were with the girls?'

Holly could see by the look on his face that he was desperate for her to be having a good time, as he was, but surely he could see that she wasn't? She wanted a quiet word with him, *just* him, but suddenly everything came pouring out before she could stop it. 'They're horrible, Dad. Really, *really* horrible. They're so rude. They're the rudest girls I've ever met. They don't want me there. They've not said a word to me. Just *about* me.' Holly was close to tears but she forced herself to hold them back.

Dad looked as if he wanted to disappear down the nearest plughole. He'd never seen Holly upset like this. But before he could speak, Cerise rose from the settee and walked over to where Holly was standing. She loomed over her. 'Almondine would never be rude to anyone. The very idea!' Cerise's eyes sparked with anger. 'How can you tell such tales? She is a very kind girl. Everybody says so.'

'That's what you think,' retorted Holly, surprising herself.

For a moment she thought Cerise might slap her. But then she turned towards Dad.

'Joe!' She appealed to him. 'Please!'

Dad was on his feet too now. His face was red and he rubbed his forehead. 'Holly, apologize at once to Cerise!'

'Why should I?' Surely he could see what was going on?

'Holly!'

'It's the truth, Dad. They were whispering about my clothes. They don't want me there.'

'Cerise?' Joe turned to her now.

'Rubbish,' snapped their hostess. 'She's oversensitive. Girls giggle about all sorts of silly things. They don't mean anything by it.'

'Yes, they do,' interrupted Holly. She was determined not to be bullied by this woman either. Sylvie cheered her on.

There was a long silence. Finally, Cerise walked towards the door. 'I think, Joe,' she said, 'that you had better go. Your daughter has been extremely rude. If she were mine, I would not tolerate that kind of behaviour for one second.'

'I'm really sorry, Cerise.' Dad looked dejected, his head bent and his shoulders hunched as he followed Cerise into the hall. For a moment Holly's temper dropped away and she felt almost sorry for him.

'He must have had high hopes,' observed Sylvie. 'Maybe he was going to ask her to marry him.'

Marry her? The idea appalled Holly. Surely not. Imagine having *Almondine* for your stepsister?

'Never mind that,' said Sylvie. 'What about having Cerise for your stepmother?'

Holly couldn't bear the thought. She'd leave home before that happened.

'Let's go,' sighed her dad as he took the damp jackets, which Cerise held out as if they were contaminated in some way. Without a word she went and fetched their shoes, handing them over in a similar fashion.

While Holly prepared herself to go back out into the rain, she saw Almondine at the top of the stairs, smiling, with Marnie smirking just behind.

Out in the car, Dad sat for a moment before turning on the ignition. His head was bowed. Holly hated to see him so miserable.

'I'm sorry, Dad.' She touched his hand. 'I couldn't help it. They were mean to me, really mean.'

'It's all right, dear. I understand. I'm not going to have you living with anyone who'd bully you.'

Holly stared at him. *Living* with! So it *had* been serious! A wave of relief swept over her. Was that what Nina had meant when she said Dad must be lonely? Suddenly the prospect of living in their flat in Leith felt like the best possible thing in the world. 'I like living with you, Dad. Just the two of us. We don't need anyone else.' She'd never told him how she felt. Perhaps she had never realised herself.

He took her hand and squeezed it. 'That's great, love. I'm glad you feel like that.' His voice was sad, though.

The rain had almost stopped but the car was steamed up. It took a few attempts to get the engine to start. Holly opened her window to let in some air and, glancing up, saw Almondine hanging out of the top window of the house. She was waving like mad. Then, when she saw that Holly had noticed, she made a rude gesture. Holly was furious, and thumbed her nose back. At that moment the front door opened and out came Cerise, striding across the pavement. She banged on the car roof. Holly's dad turned off the ignition and got out. They faced each other across the roof of the car.

'What's the matter?' he said, genuinely baffled.

'Did you see what your daughter just did?' yelled Cerise. 'Your daughter thumbed her nose at me!'

'I did not.' Holly was indignant. This was all she needed. 'It was Almondine I was being rude to, not you. And she did it first.' She didn't add that Almondine's gesture had been much worse than hers.

But Cerise paid her no attention, standing right in front of Holly's window blocking her view. Holly found herself staring directly at Cerise's midriff, which was heaving up and down.

'Did you see what she did, Joe?' repeated Cerise. 'I'm surprised you could allow your daughter to behave like that! I'm disappointed in you.'

'Good,' said Sylvie.

'This is ridiculous, Cerise.' Holly's dad didn't like to raise his voice. 'Let's leave it there, shall we?'

But Cerise was not ready to give up. 'I went to a great deal of trouble to lay on a good lunch and make your daughter feel welcome in my home.'

'I know. I appreciate that. I wish it had worked out.'

'I don't,' snorted Sylvie.

Neither did Holly.

'Let's leave it there, Cerise,' said Holly's dad again, wearily. He climbed back into the car and started the engine once again.

'Almondine did so do it first, Dad.' Holly could hear the whine in her voice, but she was determined that her dad would believe her.

'Let's forget it. OK, love? Neither of you should have been behaving like that. Let's go home.'

'Yes, let's,' agreed Sylvie. 'We've had enough of Cerise and Almondine. They've probably had enough of us too. And Cerise must be soaked, standing out there in the rain.'

The thought cheered Holly. It was the only cheering thing about the whole episode.

Four

Holly's dad was a bit low as he drove home.

'I hope he wasn't in love with her,' said Sylvie.

Not for the first time recently, Holly wished Sylvie would keep quiet.

Dad pulled up outside a chip shop. 'Fancy a fish supper?' he asked. 'I'm quite hungry, don't know about you.'

He didn't mention the horrible lunch, but Holly knew what he meant. 'I'm starved,' she said gratefully.

They both had salt and sauce – brown sauce – on their chips, and sat in the car eating contentedly. The sun had come out at last so they rolled the windows down. It was proving to be quite a nice day after all, decided Holly. Well – a nice afternoon.

'Good, aren't they?' said Dad. 'Proper chips, as they're supposed to be.'

Holly nodded. 'I am sorry, Dad,' she said, 'about thumbing my nose at Almondine, but I couldn't help it.'

He shook his head. 'If she was that rude to you –'

'She was. She really was.' Holly was still fuming at the way they had treated her. 'She and Marnie kept –'

'All right. I hear you. You can't be expected to put up with that. Though I don't approve of you thumbing your nose at anybody. And I'm sure your mum would have something to say about that kind of behaviour too.'

He hardly ever mentioned her mum. But he was right. She was a stickler for good manners, even if she wasn't very good at some other parts of being a mum. Holly was still keen to make her point. 'Almondine did it first.'

'Doesn't mean you've got to follow. I know my girl knows better than that. Let's try and forget about it.'

Holly nodded, and they didn't say any more the rest of the way home. Holly would have loved to have known what was going on inside her dad's head. He was less gloomy, now that he'd eaten his fish and chips, but he was still quite solemn. He never did spill out his thoughts in the same way as her mum, who didn't keep much back. Dad did, though. He hadn't said a word about Cerise until yesterday, for a start.

But he cheered up even more when he spotted a parking space close to their tenement. 'Pole position!' he said, as he always did when he found one of the best parking spaces.

As they opened the heavy front door into their stair they almost bumped into a woman coming out with her dog. Both she and Dad stepped back, apologizing, each taking the blame.

'You live in the top flat on the left, don't you? I'm in the one underneath you. Just moved in a couple of weeks back.'

'I hope we don't make much noise,' said Holly's dad.

'Not at all.' The woman had dark curly hair and dark eyes. Her voice was chirpy and she was smiling.

'What age do you think she is?' asked Sylvie.

Younger than Dad, Holly thought. *A bit.*

'I hope you don't hear Cindy barking,' said the woman, pointing to the dog. 'She only does it when someone goes past our door. She's really very friendly. She loves people.'

'It's not a problem,' said Holly's dad, bending down to stroke the dog's ears.

'That's good to know.'

Dad asked what breed the dog was. Holly had never realised he was interested in dogs. This one had chocolate brown, slightly curly hair and golden eyes. The woman said she was a Labradoodle, a cross between a poodle and a Labrador. They then got on to chatting about the common stair, and the weekly washing of it. Everyone was supposed to take their turn cleaning it, along with the passage in the basement that led to the drying green, but some didn't do their share. It was exactly the same in Mum's place. Holly's dad always did his section and it seemed that their new neighbour was the same.

'By the way,' she said, 'I'm Anna.' She held out her hand.

'Joe,' responded Holly's dad, and they shook hands. 'And this is my daughter, Holly. She lives with me.'

'Hello, Holly,' said Anna, giving her a wide smile.

'Hello,' said Holly, and smiled back politely to show her dad she really did know better than to act like Almondine.

'You must be on holiday?' said Anna. 'So am I! School holidays.' She explained that she taught art at a high school, the one Holly would go to next term.

Dad looked pleased. 'It'll be nice for you to know one of the teachers, won't it, Holly?'

Holly nodded. She wasn't very good at art.

'Better be on my way then,' said Anna. 'Cindy's dying for a walk, aren't you, girl? Nice to meet you both.'

'You, too,' said Dad. He held the stair door open for them.

Holly and her dad climbed the three flights of stairs. He puffed a little as they made their way up the final flight.

'We'll start looking for a new place soon,' he promised, just as he always did. Holly often wondered why. She had never complained about his flat. It might not feel quite like home yet, but it was getting there.

As they reached the top landing the door of the flat opposite theirs opened and out came Mrs McGinty. She was one of the reasons Dad wanted to move. Little happened that got past her.

'I thought I heard folk talking down there.' She spoke sharply. 'Was it that woman below?' Mrs McGinty continued. 'The one with the dog? Dogs shouldn't be allowed on a common stair.'

'It doesn't bark much,' said Dad. He generally tried to avoid getting into conversation with their nosy neighbour.

'I've heard it. Yapping.'

At that moment Holly's mobile rang. She pulled it out of her pocket. It wasn't a number she recognized, but when she answered it she heard her mum's voice, all the way from Tenerife. She turned to her dad, mouthing, 'It's Mum!' and he gently pushed her towards the flat door, unlocking it for her.

'Hello, Mum!' Holly couldn't help smiling, eager to listen to her mum chatter away about her holiday, the meals she'd eaten and the people she'd met. It was great to hear her on such good form. 'Is it sunny there, Mum? It's not here. It's been raining most of the day. What are you doing now?'

Her mum started to say something then paused for a moment. 'Hang on . . . Lenny says it costs a fortune to phone the UK. I'm on his mobile. Mine's run out of money. I'd better get off, hen, but I just wanted to say hello. I'll see you soon. Lots of love. A big hug.'

'A big hug,' said Holly in return but her mum had already cut the call. It was hard not to feel a bit flat.

'It's that Lenny!' said Sylvie. 'Why does she always do what he tells her?'

Holly didn't know the answer to that.

'Yes, that'll be her mother,' Dad was saying to Mrs McGinty in the hall.

'I hope you're never going to let her go back to live with that besom,' Holly heard her say. What right did that woman have to talk about her mum like that?

'Excuse me, Mrs McGinty,' said her dad, speaking very politely, 'if you'd just let me past?'

He opened the door of their flat and came inside, shaking his head. 'She's a menace,' he muttered. He noticed that Holly's call had ended. 'That was short and sweet. How's your mum?'

'Great,' said Holly. 'She's having a good time.'

'That's nice, love.' He never sounded comfortable when talking about her mum. 'Good of her to ring.'

Holly nodded. 'I'd love to go to Tenerife sometime, Dad,' she said. 'Mum says she'll take me one day.'

'One day,' echoed her dad.

'She will! I know she will.'

'I'm sure you do.' He put the kettle on. 'I'm going to go to the Property Centre tomorrow to see what they've got,' he said, changing the subject. 'A wee bungalow would be nice, wouldn't it?'

'Not in Portobello,' said Holly before she could stop herself. She felt a bit mean now that she'd spoilt his day. 'I'm sorry, Dad,' she said, as she had before. It wasn't really her fault though, was it? She shouldn't have had to put up with Almondine and Marnie sniggering at her, making her feel like a piece of rubbish, should she?

'Of course not,' said Sylvie.

'It's all right, love,' said her dad heavily. 'I don't imagine we'll be visiting Cerise again. I can see it wouldn't have worked out.'

'It certainly would not,' agreed Sylvie. 'What he was thinking about, taking up with a woman like that? She'd have bossed him to bits. You've saved him from a dreadful fate.'

The thought comforted Holly. He'd had a narrow escape. As had she.

Five

As it turned out, Holly had been too quick in thinking about escapes, narrow or otherwise.

When she was getting ready to go out the next morning the phone rang. Dad had just rushed down the stairs to work and Holly thought the caller might be Johnny, asking when she was coming round to his house. It wasn't.

'Oh, hello, is that you, Holly?'

'Yes.' The line was a bit woolly and Holly couldn't quite make out the voice. Maybe it was somebody from the Social Services checking up? She felt herself stiffen.

'This is Cerise.'

Holly goggled at herself in the hall mirror. She couldn't believe it! With everything that had gone on yesterday she was sure Cerise had been put off for good. 'Dad's gone to work,' she said quickly.

'I thought he would have. No, it was you I wanted to speak to. I was thinking about you being all on your own there.'

Holly decided against mentioning Sylvie. She said nothing.

'I just wanted to say how much I enjoyed meeting you yesterday.'

Holly made another face at herself in the mirror. Had

she heard Cerise correctly?

'Liar,' said Sylvie.

'Almondine, too,' Cerise went on. 'She was just saying she'd love to get to know you a bit better.'

Holly couldn't think what to say.

'Are you still there, dear?'

'Yes.'

'Almondine said it was rather difficult yesterday with Marnie being there. Marnie can be a bit, well – how should I put it? Yes – Marnie can be just a teeny bit funny at times,' said Cerise. 'You know what I mean? And maybe a teensy bit jealous?'

Holly could think of nothing to say to that either.

'Anyway, Holly,' Cerise went on, her voice as smooth as melted chocolate, 'we were wondering, with it being the school holidays, and your dad out at work all day, if you'd like to come over and spend the day with Almondine?'

Spend the day with that dreadful girl? Horror of horrors!

'Well –' began Holly, desperately trying to find the words she wanted, but Cerise cut her off.

'I could come over now and collect you in the car. It'd be no trouble. My first client's not due in until ten.'

'Erm . . .' Holly's stomach was churning. Cerise had it all planned. What could she say?

'Would you fancy that, Holly?' asked Cerise. 'The sun's out today. It'll be lovely down on the beach. You could bring your swimming things.'

'I'm sorry,' said Holly. 'I'm afraid I can't. I'm going over to my friend Johnny's house in a wee while. His mum's asked me to lunch.'

Cerise cut in again. 'Oh. I didn't realise, but you could still come here for an hour or so and I'll drop you off at your friend's house.' She was sounding less plummy now. She obviously didn't like not getting her own way.

'Sorry, I've got my friend Sylvie popping in this morning, you see.' Holly panicked.

'Too bad.' Cerise sounded a bit down in the dumps. 'Another day then?' It seemed she was not going to be easily put off.

'Maybe,' mumbled Holly.

'What about tomorrow?'

'I'm staying the night at Johnny's house. I'm not sure what time I'll be back.' The words tumbled out of Holly's mouth. She hated being a liar, but with Cerise you'd have to be or else she'd flatten you like a steamroller.

'That's a great pity. We'll have to sort something out for another day.' Cerise's voice had turned sharp.

'Well,' said Holly. 'I think maybe . . .'

But Cerise was determined. 'I'll give you a call in a day or two, then. To make an arrangement with your dad. Be sure to tell him I phoned, won't you?'

Holly didn't bother to reply to that, as she had no intention of telling her dad.

'Don't forget! Bye for now then, dear,' said Cerise and Holly replaced the receiver. The phone call had given her a jolt. Cerise was obviously not going to give Dad up that quickly.

The next shock was arriving at the Nightingales' house to find Johnny in the back garden with a stranger. They were bouncing a ball between them and catching it in an idle kind of way.

'That's Lauren,' said Nina. 'She's just come to live next door.'

Holly froze.

'She's a nice girl,' added Nina. 'Her dad's a doctor too, like Colin. He's come to work in the same practice. I hope you'll be friends with her. She's about your age. Perhaps a little older. Twelve, I think.'

And Johnny was thirteen.

What was she so bothered about? She wasn't Johnny's *girlfriend*, she was his friend. They were more like brother and sister really. But now Lauren had been added to the mix and Holly didn't like things to change when they'd been going on nice and smoothly. She turned to Nina and began to help dry some dishes. She needed a bit of time before she joined Johnny and Lauren in the garden.

'How did it go yesterday?' asked Nina as she chopped vegetables.

Holly grimaced.

'Oh, I see. It was like that, was it?' Nina smiled. 'Tell me about this . . . friend of your dad's.'

'She was awful.'

'You can't sum a person up on one meeting, surely.'

'You wouldn't like her, Nina,' said Holly. 'Really you wouldn't.'

But they were interrupted by Johnny, calling to Holly from the garden.

Nina led the way out. 'Oh well, you can tell me all about it later. Come on out now and meet Lauren. I think you'll like *her*.'

The Nightingales lived in a large stone Victorian house on the other side of town from Holly. It had a walled garden with a couple of apple trees and a fantastic monkey puzzle tree, as well as masses of flowers in all the borders. It was not overly tidy – nor was the house, in fact – but Holly loved it. She had never lived in a house with a garden. Her dad said they'd have one if he bought a bungalow. *If*.

'Hi, Holly!' Johnny greeted her. 'We could finish that game of chess if you'd like.' He was crazy about chess and had taught her to play when they first became friends. 'Are you up for it?'

She nodded and relaxed a little.

'Johnny,' said his mother, 'do you have to play chess today of all days? It's a lovely sunny morning, too good to be indoors. And there are three of you – chess is no good for three.'

'It's all right, I have to go back home in a minute,' said Lauren cheerfully.

'And I don't mind,' put in Holly quickly. She'd like nothing better than to go inside with Johnny and leave the strange girl in the garden.

'But, Mum,' protested Johnny, 'I'll be out all afternoon, Tim said he'd call round and we'd play tennis.'

Holly sighed inwardly. He hadn't mentioned that.

Nina turned to the girl. 'Lauren,' she said, 'this is our friend Holly. We were telling you about her yesterday.'

Holly was alarmed. What had Nina told Lauren? That her mum had dumped her on Nina in Queen Street Station in Glasgow one afternoon and then flitted off on holiday? That her mum worked in a club in Glasgow called the *Silver Spike* and didn't come home until two in the morning. That her mum lived with a horrible man called Lenny? That her dad had had to give up his job in the Middle East to come home and look after her?

Why was she being so jumpy? Holly knew Nina would never let her down.

'Hi, Holly,' said Lauren. 'Nice to meet you. Nina says you've moved to Edinburgh quite recently too.'

Lauren had thick brown hair cut neatly round her ears and she was at least three inches taller than Holly. She spoke smoothly and politely, perfectly at ease. She probably went to the same school as Johnny, and his friend Tim. Holly hated being the outsider.

'Hello,' she said, not looking at Lauren directly.

'I'll go in and get the chess board set up,' said Johnny and off he went.

'I'll leave you two girls to get to know each other,' said Nina and she followed Johnny indoors.

Lauren perched on the arm of one of the benches. She seemed very much at home for somebody who didn't know the Nightingales very well. Holly, who did, stood about awkwardly, shifting from foot to foot.

'How long have you known Johnny?' asked Lauren.

'About three months.' Holly couldn't believe it! Only three months? She felt as if the Nightingales had been in her life for years.

Lauren looked surprised. 'Oh, is that all? By the way Johnny talked about you I thought you'd known him forever.'

That pleased Holly. Lauren obviously didn't know how Holly had come to meet the Nightingales. Nina could keep secrets better than anyone she knew. It wasn't that Holly was ashamed of what had happened, but Lauren didn't look as if she'd ever get abandoned in a railway station, so there was no way she would have understood.

'Holly,' yelled Johnny from the back door. 'I've got the board set up.'

'Coming,' Holly shouted back, relieved. She smiled shyly at Lauren. 'Better go,' she said.

'Holly,' began Lauren, 'would you like to come round to my place this afternoon? While Johnny and Tim are playing tennis?'

'Holly,' yelled Johnny again from the house.

'Gosh, he's impatient,' said Lauren, laughing. 'So, will you come?' she asked again. 'I'd like you to.'

'Oh, OK, yes, thanks.' Holly felt herself blushing.

'Whenever you like after lunch. See you then.'

Why on earth had Holly agreed? She didn't want to spend the afternoon with a complete stranger! She walked back to the house. Johnny was hovering in the kitchen where Nina was making soup.

'You didn't have to shout,' teased Holly.

'You're quite right, Holly,' said Nina. 'I'm always ticking him off for it as well. He's got a voice like a foghorn these days.'

Johnny groaned. 'Come on then,' he said to Holly. 'Let's go!'

They played the chess game in the dining room, on the long mahogany table. It took them nearly two hours to finish and Holly won. She didn't often win against Johnny.

He shook his head, annoyed with himself, then said a bit reluctantly, 'Well done, Hol.' For once he didn't try to make any excuses.

When they went back to the kitchen Holly couldn't resist telling Nina.

'No need to brag about it,' said Johnny.

'Why shouldn't she?' demanded Nina with a smile. 'You would. Congratulations, Holly! Johnny needs to be beaten once in a while. Does him good.'

Johnny grimaced.

The door opened and in came Colin, Johnny's father. He had only a short break for lunch between surgeries. He greeted Holly and they all sat down to eat at the round wooden table.

'How's it going, Holly?' he asked.

'Fine.' She couldn't help telling him, too, about her chess triumph.

As soon as Johnny had finished eating he jumped up and said that, since Holly wasn't coming, he'd go early and meet Tim. 'I'm going to thrash him this afternoon,' he told them, miming a winning shot across the kitchen as he left.

Shortly afterwards, Colin excused himself and went back to work.

Holly helped Nina stack the dishwasher. She liked these private moments with Nina, just the two of them together.

Holly told her the story of her lunch with Cerise and Almondine and how Cerise had rung that morning and tried to bully her into spending the day with them.

'That's what she is, a bully!'

'Certainly sounds a bit like it.' Nina was more sympathetic now she had heard the whole story. 'But I really don't think you need to worry. I can't see your dad falling for a woman like that. He's too level-headed. He wouldn't go into anything lightly.'

That cheered Holly. Nina was a good judge of character. They could leave Cerise behind now and talk of other things, like Nina's new book.

'How are you getting on with it?' asked Holly.

'Slowly. But I think it's going to work out.'

Nina wrote children's books, books that Holly loved. She particularly liked the series that had a character called Sylvie in them. That was how her own Sylvie had come into being. Not that she'd ever told Nina. Or anybody else for that matter – her parents avoid asking much about Sylvie and Holly didn't especially want to tell them.

Holly often thought she would like to be a writer when she grew up, if she was good enough that was.

'You could be a writer now,' Nina was always telling her. 'Don't judge yourself too hard. Just get on and do it. The more you practice, the better you'll get.'

Holly had made a start on a novel when she came to

live in Edinburgh, but she hadn't shown it to anyone yet. It was probably rubbish, she'd decided. She couldn't help wondering if Lauren was good at writing stories and whether Nina talked to her about her books too.

'So what would you like to do this afternoon?' asked Nina, interrupting Holly's worries. 'I must go to my study and get my head down. I've set myself a deadline!'

'Lauren – the girl from next door – has asked me round.'

'Oh, I am pleased,' said Nina. 'She's a very nice girl and she likes books, so I'm sure you'll get on just fine with her, if you let yourself,' she added with a smile.

Holly didn't feel at all comfortable about that. She was thinking of making an excuse not to go. She'd rather stay at Nina's and read a book.

'I'm not sure . . .'

'Go! Go!' encouraged Nina. 'I'll see you later on.'

And so Holly, with a weak feeling in her stomach, went next door.

Six

Lauren's mother opened the door to Holly's rather timid knock. Holly hadn't been sure whether she should use the brass door knocker shaped like a lion's head or ring the bell. She had decided to try the knocker first. Nothing happened for a minute or two and she was wondering whether to ring the bell when the door opened and a woman came out.

'I thought there was someone at the door but I wasn't sure. I was in the kitchen. You must be Holly?'

Holly nodded.

'Come on in then. I'm Lauren's mum – she told me you were coming. Just call me Avril.'

Holly couldn't imagine doing that. Avril was smartly dressed and made-up, unlike Nina who wore jeans most of the time with a loose shirt or a sweater over them. She said it didn't matter what writers wore when they were working. They were alone, shut away from the world.

'Lauren!' Avril stood at the foot of the stairs. 'It's Holly.'

Lauren appeared on the top landing and leaned over the banisters. 'Want to come up, Holly?'

Holly began to climb the stairs. It was a big house with lots of rooms, like the Nightingales' next door.

'Come in,' said Lauren, leading the way into her bedroom.

It was a large sunny room, with yellow walls and a blue ceiling. The curtains and the downie cover were patterned in blue and yellow to match, much nicer than Almondine's horrible room.

'Do you like it?' asked Lauren. 'I was allowed to choose the colours myself.'

'It's lovely,' said Holly. She must get her dad to help her decorate her room. At the moment it had porridgey-coloured wallpaper, with little pale lilac flowers dotted around, that had been put up by the previous owners. Dad had promised she could choose her own colours when they moved, but Holly thought there was no use waiting till he got his bungalow. She might wait for ever.

'Glad you like it,' said Lauren, smiling.

'Anyone would,' replied Holly.

The room looked down into the back garden. You could see the Nightingales' garden, too, from here. It was empty at the moment but for a ginger cat lying along a branch of one of the apple trees.

'Would you like to have a look at my books?' asked Lauren. 'Nina says you read a lot.'

One wall was covered with books. Holly had read a good many of them, though not all, of course, and she owned only a few. She went to the library most weeks.

The girls started chatting about books and other things and before long Holly learned that Lauren and her family had just moved up from London.

'I don't know anyone in Edinburgh. It all feels a bit odd,' Lauren confessed. 'I didn't want to leave London. All my friends are there and now I'll have to go to a new school in September where everybody will already have their own friends.'

Holly could sympathise with that. She'd been through the same kind of thing herself last term when she'd moved to Edinburgh from Glasgow. Her dad said it would be easier for her next year. It just took time to adjust, she assured Lauren.

After a while Lauren suggested going down into the garden where her mother gave them tall glasses of homemade lemonade and chocolate ginger biscuits. And so the afternoon passed far more easily and pleasantly than Holly had imagined.

But she was still relieved when Johnny returned home. She and Lauren were sitting chatting on a rug on the lawn – they heard his voice before they saw him. He put his head over the wall and yelled, 'Holly, Mum wants to know if you're staying at ours for supper?'

'If that's all right,' replied Holly.

'She wouldn't ask you if it wasn't. Idiot!' With that, Johnny dropped from their sight.

'He doesn't mean to be rude,' said Holly. 'That's just Johnny.'

'He's nice though, isn't he?'

Holly shrugged. 'He's OK.' She'd never have called Johnny *nice*. Not exactly. She got up and thanked Lauren for having her.

'Come again, dear,' said Avril when she saw Holly leaving. 'It's so nice for Lauren to have your company.'

Holly hadn't thought of it like that. But she knew that it wouldn't be long before Lauren had lots of new friends.

Holly had a good evening with the Nightingales. Johnny was in high spirits as he'd beaten Tim at tennis and Colin told them stories about his escapades when he was a teenager. He even brought out old photos of himself aged thirteen, all gawky looking with long hair well down past his shoulders. He made everybody laugh. If you'd seen him then you'd never have thought he'd become a doctor.

Nina drove Holly home afterwards. Dad liked her to be home by nine at the latest. As Nina pulled up by Holly's front door she said, peering through the windscreen, 'Who's that on the pavement talking to your dad?'

Holly looked. 'It's my mum!' she cried. 'What's she doing here? I thought she was still in Tenerife.' She opened the car door and jumped out.

'Mum!' she shouted.

Sharon came running towards her, swaying a little on her high heels, her blonde ponytail flying behind her. They collided in each other's arms.

'I thought you were in Tenerife, Mum.'

'We got into Edinburgh a couple of hours ago. I thought I'd come down and see if your dad would let me take you take you home to Glasgow with me, just for a night or two, since it's the school holidays. I haven't seen you for ages.'

Holly's dad joined them.

'Dad, can I go and stay with Mum in Glasgow?'

He looked furious and for a second Holly wondered

if *she* had upset him. Perhaps Cerise had called?

'Please!' pleaded Holly, but Dad shook his head.

'Sharon, why do you do this? You know you can't take her. Not to your house.'

'But Dad,' wailed Holly. 'I want to go! *Please*!' She hadn't seen her mum in weeks.

'Listen, Joe,' said Sharon, 'I told you, I've finished with Lenny.'

'Since when?'

'We broke up this morning. At the airport in Tenerife. I came straight here.'

'This morning! And I'm supposed to believe that's the end of it?' His laugh was harsh.

'It is, Joe. I'm not having him back this time.'

'We'll need to wait and see about that.'

Holly knew her dad was right. She didn't want him to be right, but he was. Her mum had broken up with Lenny before and they'd always got back together. But she still wanted to go with her mum, even just for the one night.

'It'll be all right with the Social Services as long as Lenny's not there,' said Sharon.

'No, it will not be all right,' said Dad firmly. He could be so stubborn when he wanted. 'There's still your job at the *Silver Spike*, remember? Going on until all hours of the morning. And Holly left on her own.'

'But I won't be working tonight,' said Sharon. 'I wouldn't have asked otherwise. I'll be in with her all night. Anyway, I'm going to get another job, Joe. Honest I am. In a cafe, as a waitress, finishing early.'

'I've heard all that before,' retorted Dad. 'There is no question of Holly going back with you tonight. Or any other night. She is well settled in with me now.'

Her mum began to cry – and her crying became noisy. She and Dad were attracting attention. Passers-by were turning to look at them.

Nina came over. 'Everything OK?' she asked, in her calm voice.

'Mum,' said Holly, 'this is Nina. She's been wanting to meet you.'

'We did meet briefly!' Nina smiled at Sharon. 'At the station in Glasgow. Remember?'

'Oh yes, so we did! You were the kind lady who offered to look after Holly that time. I didn't recognize you there.' Sharon wiped her eyes with her sleeve.

They'd met only for a minute that afternoon before Sharon had fled along the station platform, worried about being late for work. And Nina had not *offered*. Holly had been dumped on her. Holly felt embarrassed as her mum carried on.

'I was ever so grateful to you,' said Sharon to Nina. 'I knew she'd be safe with you seein' as you'd been at her school and wrote books. I wouldn't have let her go with just anybody. You can't be too careful. She says she sees quite a bit of you, now that she's living here . . . in Edinburgh.'

'It is always a pleasure to have Holly,' said Nina. 'She's welcome any time.'

'She calls you her fairy godmother.' Sharon sniffed.

'That's nice to know.'

Holly was beginning to feel awkward. So, she could see, was her dad.

'I think we should go upstairs and have a talk,' he said finally. 'Come on then, Holly. Sharon?'

'I'll head home now,' said Nina. 'Nice to meet you again,' she added to Sharon.

'Thanks a lot, Nina,' said Dad. He shrugged, embarrassed.

'I'll see you soon, Holly.' Nina gave her a quick hug before returning to her car. For two pennies, Holly would have run after her, but knew she couldn't.

They climbed the stairs in silence but for the click-clack of Sharon's heels and the occasional puff emitted by Holly's dad. Holly had once told him he should go to the gym. That's what Colin did. But Dad said he'd no space left in his life, by the time he got home from work, had done the shopping and cooking and sorted out the washing. Holly helped a bit but, as she would admit herself, not an awful lot.

For once, Mrs McGinty was not at her door. She must be watching television. They could hear it since she had the sound turned up as usual.

Holly's dad unlocked the flat door and they went inside, the three of them.

Seven

Holly went and sat on her bed for a few minutes. She could hear her parents talking in the living room. She couldn't hear exactly what they were saying but at least they weren't shouting now. She even heard Mum give one of her giggles. Once she was sure that they weren't going to row, she went through to join them.

They were sitting together on the sofa, looking at Dad's calendar, noting down the days that her mum wasn't working. Everything seemed quite calm. Dad was talking in his usual quiet voice and Mum sounded relaxed and happier. For the first time in ages, Holly wondered whether it might be possible for them to live together. They seemed to be getting on pretty well with each other, her mum and her dad. They turned and smiled at her.

'Cup of tea, Sharon?' Dad went to put on the kettle.

But all was not well. The minute he was out the room, Sharon suddenly burst into tears.

Holly put her arms around her shoulders. 'It's all right, Mum.'

'He told me to get lost!' wailed Sharon.

'Who?' Surely not Dad!

'Lenny, of course.'

Not him again. 'Mum, you're better off without him. You say that yourself.'

'But I want to be with him. I hate being on my own.'

Hadn't she just told Dad out there on the pavement that she was giving up Lenny for good? What was she playing at? But Holly couldn't bear to see her mum so unhappy. She hugged her as tight as she could.

When Dad came back with the tea he shook his head, as if it was beyond him trying to understand. 'One minute you say you never want to see him again. The next . . .' He threw up his hands.

'I know, I know!' said Sharon. She took several deep breaths. 'I'm sure I've got a hankie in my case. And a fresh T-shirt. Could you fetch them for me, love?'

'Where is your case, Mum?' asked Holly. She hadn't seen any sign of it, just the big tote bag that her mum always carried.

'Oh no!' Mum slapped the palm of her hand against her forehead. 'Lenny took it off the carousel at the airport.'

'So where is it now?' asked Dad.

'Don't know. With Lenny, most likely.'

'So he's a thief as well as everything else,' said Holly. That didn't surprise her. 'Fancy stealing your luggage!'

'He didn't steal it. He's not a thief. He probably thought I wouldn't be able to manage the weight.' Mum couldn't bear to hear a word against Lenny. It had always been the same.

She can't still love him, thought Holly. *Surely she's not that daft.* Usually Sylvie would say something on the matter, but she remained quiet too.

Her mum cried a bit more, sniffled and drank her tea,

and gradually calmed down again. She told Holly about her holiday whilst Dad went to buy a carry-out. He came back with a large pizza, which he and Sharon shared. Holly wasn't hungry after eating earlier at Nina's.

'Didn't you eat before, Dad?' Holly asked. 'Remember there were the leftovers from last night?'

'Didn't get round to it. I went to the pub earlier on for a drink.'

'By yourself?' Holly hoped he hadn't met up with Cerise.

'With that woman downstairs. The one with the dog. What's her name now? Anna?'

Holly said nothing. She didn't know how she felt about this new development.

But her mum did. 'Have you got yourself a girlfriend then, Joe?'

'No, I have not. She's a neighbour. We just happened to bump into each other on the stairs.' He cleared the plates away in the kitchen.

When Dad came back he asked Holly to go into her room for a minute. He said he wanted to have a chat with her mother in private.

'Why can't I stay? I know what you're going to talk about.'

'Just go, Holly, please. OK?' Her dad was at the end of his tether, Holly realised that.

Holly went, but after her dad had closed the door she crept back into the hall and put her ear against it. It was easy enough to hear them as their voices were soon raised.

'I want Holly back, Joe. To stay with me.'

'You know it's not on, Sharon.'

'Girls need their mothers.'

'I'm her dad and I think she needs me to see she has proper food in her stomach and gets out to school on time in the mornings.'

'I did all that.'

'Did you really? What I heard was that you went to bed at three o'clock in the morning, and slept in so that Holly had to get herself out to school.'

'I couldn't help it, Joe. It was my job. You were good sending me money, I know, but we needed a few extras.'

'You didn't have to take a job that kept you out half the night! Not when you'd a child to look after.'

'But I told you, if I can get a different job, a day job, and Lenny's not staying with me –'

'If, if, if! I'm sick of hearing that word. Do you think I can believe anything you tell me? You've just been weeping all over our daughter, telling her how much you're missing him.'

'I won't let him come back, Joe. Promise, cross my heart. And I will get another job. Give me a chance. I'll show you.'

'Look, Sharon, Holly's happy here. She's got friends, good friends. The Nightingales' place is like another home for her. She can go there when I'm working. And when I'm not, we spend plenty of time together.'

'She can have a home with me too, Joe.'

Sharon started to cry again and Holly wanted to go in and comfort her but knew that if she did her dad would lose his rag. His voice was getting unusually loud.

'But you're never in, Sharon, even when you're not working. You can't stay in the house for more than ten minutes, I know you!'

The catch on the door opened abruptly and Holly almost fell into the room. Her dad stood there glaring at her.

'Can you never do what you're told?' he barked.

'She does what I tell her,' put in Sharon. 'Don't you, pet?'

Holly stood, mute. She didn't want to agree or disagree with either one of them.

'You might as well come in, Holly,' sighed Dad. 'You'll have heard it all, I'm sure.'

Holly went in and all three sat down again.

'Let's be calm about this,' said Dad and gave Holly's shoulder an apologetic squeeze.

Sharon turned to Holly. 'You like it with me, don't you?'

'Yes,' said Holly. Her mum was good fun. There always seemed to be something exciting going on when she was around.

'There you are, Joe!'

'But I like being with my dad too,' added Holly. 'He's good to me. I like it here. And you are really busy, Mum.'

'She could at least spend weekends with me, Joe,' said Sharon. 'That's not asking much.'

Dad studied his knees for a while. '*If* you get another job, we'll see about it,' he said quietly. 'But it's not on while you're coming home from the *Spike* at three in the morning. And *definitely* not if Lenny's around. And we'll have to clear it with the social worker too.'

Sharon gave one of her wide smiles, as if everything was sorted now. 'I'll start looking for another job right away. And I'll tell Lenny where to go if he tries to come near.' She seemed to have forgotten her earlier tears for her lost boyfriend.

'We'll wait till that happens.' Dad sounded tired now. He glanced at his watch. 'I think you've missed the last train to Glasgow . . .'

Sharon looked at her watch and jumped up. 'You're right, Joe. I have. What am I going to do?'

'I suppose you'd better stay the night here.' Dad didn't sound too pleased with the idea but he had no choice.

'That'd be great, Joe. If you don't mind?'

'I'm not going to see you sleeping in the street, am I? And I shouldn't think you've much money left after your holiday?'

'You know what it's like when you're away – you spend the lot! More than you think.' Sharon gave one of her little giggles.

Dad made no comment. He was careful with his money. 'There's an extra bed in Holly's room,' he said.

It was like having a sleepover with her mum. They gossiped and giggled until all hours.

Sharon had picked up a couple of holiday brochures someone had left lying about at the airport. She was full of ideas as to where they might go, just her and Holly together. They lay on their tummies, turning the pages, carried away by the photos of turquoise swimming pools and lovely white beaches.

50

'How would you fancy Turkey, love?' Mum said.

Holly fancied going anywhere in the world. Anywhere foreign. Different from here. Not that she didn't like Edinburgh, but she'd never been abroad.

'Chrissie – you ken Chrissie, my pal at the *Spike*? – she's going to Lanzarote. Pick a place! Anywhere in the world!'

Holly closed her eyes. 'Disneyland!' she said, finally. She wasn't completely sure that would be her dream holiday, but she knew that her mum would love it.

'That would be fun. We could go to L.A. too. We could see the stars in Hollywood.' Sharon laughed and so did Holly.

'Nina says Venice is magical,' suggested Holly.

'Does she?' said Mum, suddenly subdued. 'It's not really my kind of holiday . . .'

Holly regretted having mentioned Nina to her mum, but her good mood returned almost immediately.

Lanzarote, Disneyland, Venice . . . There was no end to the places they could go to.

Mum was still looking through the brochure when Holly drifted off into dreamland.

In the morning, when she wakened, the other bed was empty. Her mum had gone, leaving a note on the bedside table.

See you soon in Glasgow, pet. Love Mum x

Eight

Holly felt kind of squashed after she'd read her mum's note, as if someone had sat on her. Her dad got ready to go off to work as usual.

'Hate leaving you, love, but no option I'm afraid. Need to earn a crust.' He was using up some of his annual leave, taking every other Friday off so they could spend more time together and Dad had mentioned a week away later in the year. Holly wouldn't mind if they ended up staying in Edinburgh. Holidays were expensive.

'I know, Dad.'

'Are you sure you're all right on your own all day? I could ask –' He stopped. Perhaps he'd been going to say 'Cerise'. Holly hadn't told him about the phone call the previous day.

'Of course I'll be all right,' she told him brightly. Most days she went to the Nightingales' but they were going to visit Johnny's grandmother in Perth today. It was his granny's birthday and they would be gone until evening.

'I'm off then, love,' said her dad. He came and kissed her on the forehead. 'Phone me if you need me. And remember to take your key and some of the money from the tin if you go out anywhere. I'll be back by six, I promise. And I'll give you a call on your mobile at lunch time as usual.'

'Dad —' Holly caught hold of his hand as he walked by, 'do you hate Mum?'

'No, of course not. We're just too different to live together. You know that, don't you?' He gave his head a little shake. She could see he didn't like talking about it. He dropped another quick kiss on the top of her head. 'See you later!'

The door closed behind him. Holly went to the window and watched him walking towards his car, getting in and taking off. She always felt a bit lonely at that moment.

'You've got me,' Sylvie reminded her.

Holly smiled to herself. Yesterday had been so hectic that Sylvie had hardly been able to get a word in. It was good to have her back.

The day was bright and Holly hated being cooped up in the flat on her own so after a while she ran down the stairs into the sunshine. She dawdled up the street looking in the windows. Some shops were open, others still had their shutters down.

When she heard her name being called she turned. Anna was coming towards her with Cindy straining at the leash.

'Hello there, Holly,' said Anna. 'Cindy and I are out for our morning walk. Your dad'll be away to work?'

Holly nodded. She rubbed Cindy's ears.

'Want to join us?' Anna asked.

'OK.' Holly nodded. Anna seemed nice enough.

'I thought we might walk into Leith. I often go down there and have a coffee looking over the water.'

They fell into step and headed for the port. Cindy

trotted beside them, stopping every now and then whenever she met another dog to exchange greetings. Anna seemed to know all the owners, but she told Holly she didn't know any of their names, just the names of their dogs.

It was still fairly quiet around the port, though a few of the many cafes and restaurants were opening up. They found one with outside tables. Anna said she was going to have coffee and a croissant.

'What about you, Holly? Fancy a hot chocolate? And a croissant?'

Holly fancied both. She accepted shyly. After all, she scarcely knew Anna.

'You've got quite a tan, Holly,' remarked Anna while they waited for their order. 'Suits you. You must have been outside a lot.'

'She's sooking up,' warned Sylvie. 'You've not really got that much of a tan.'

'I've been in my friend's garden,' explained Holly. And she'd been on the tennis courts with Johnny a few times, but preferred not to remember that.

'Your dad tells me you read a lot? What have you got on the go at present?'

'*Journey to the River Sea*. A friend at school lent it to me. It's good. It's by Eva Ibbotson.'

They talked about the book for a few minutes and then Holly could sense Anna steering the conversation round to her dad.

'I had a nice drink with him yesterday evening.'

'He said.'

'We seem to have the same sense of humour.' Anna smiled at the recollection of some joke she must have shared with Holly's father.

Alarm bells were ringing in Holly's head. They were going off a lot these days.

'You must be on your own often? Your dad goes out quite early, doesn't he?'

'Just after eight usually. Same time as me in term time.' Holly paused, then said, 'We were up late last night. My mum was through from Glasgow.'

Anna's eyes widened. 'I thought they didn't see each other any more? Your dad said –'

'She stayed the night, my mum did. They're talking about getting back together again, she and my dad.'

'Holly Hamilton,' said Sylvie, 'you should be struck down dead where you stand. That was a right whopper!'

'You'll be pleased about that then?'

Holly looked carefully at Anna and nodded.

'Do you think she fancies your dad?' asked Sylvie. 'She'd be a better choice than Cerise.'

Dad didn't need anyone, in Holly's opinion. They were fine together, just the two of them. If he'd got back together with her mum, well, that would be different.

'No point waiting for that to happen,' said Sylvie.

But today Holly wasn't going to take everything Sylvie said as a fact.

After they'd sat a while and finished their drinks and croissants Anna roused Cindy, who had gone to sleep in a pool of sunlight, and said, 'I must make a move. I'm planning to drive down the coast and do some painting.'

'That sounds nice,' said Holly.

'Would you like to come with me one day? You might try a little painting too. Your dad says you draw well.'

Holly shrugged. 'Not really. Not very well.' She didn't like the idea of her dad talking about her to other people. Although wasn't *she* doing just that, talking about him?

'Look, Holly,' said Anna, 'I know you're on your own a lot –'

'I'm fine,' Holly cut in quickly. 'I don't mind being on my own.'

'I'm sure you don't, but think about it. You can ring my bell any time. You know where to find me.' Anna smiled.

'She's really quite nice,' said Sylvie. 'She means well. You might think about it.'

But today Holly could think only about her mum.

☆ ☆ ☆

Holly waited until lunchtime after Dad had called to check she was all right, and then she phoned her mum.

'Oh hi, Holly, pet.' Sharon yawned. 'I was asleep. What are you up to?'

'Nothing.'

'Nothing?'

'Dad's at work. He'll be away all day.'

'And he complains about me leaving you!'

'But he's not away till three in the morning,' Sylvie pointed out.

Holly wished she'd shut up. Sylvie could get on her

nerves at times – she had an opinion on everything, like a fly buzzing around her ear.

'Why don't you come on through to Glasgow? We could spend the afternoon together. Go shopping.'

Holly's dislike of going on the train alone was outweighed by the excitement she felt at her mum's suggestion. She hadn't been shopping with her mum in months. 'I'd like to but –'

'But what?'

'Dad –'

'You'd be home before him.'

'I'm not sure –'

'Oh, come on, Holly! Let's have some fun. He won't eat you. This isn't breaking any of your dad's rules, is it?'

'Well –' Holly was still hesitating. She was pretty sure it was . . .

'Have you enough money for the fare?'

'I think so. Yes, I should have.' Dad always left her with money for emergencies. She could use that.

'You could get the two o'clock, be here at a quarter to three. I'll meet you at the station. Buy you a late lunch. We could have a couple of hours together and you could get the 4.30 back and be home before your dad. He'll never know!' Mum sounded delighted with her plan. 'What do you say, love?'

What could Holly say? The offer was too tempting and she had nothing else planned.

'OK . . .'

'Great!' said Sharon. 'See you at the station!' And she rang off.

'I hope Dad won't kill me,' thought Holly. All of a sudden her stomach clenched with worry.

'He needn't know,' said Sylvie. 'Like your mum said. Anyway, we could do with an adventure. We haven't had one for a while.'

Sylvie loved adventures. In Nina's books she often got caught up in an adventure of one kind or another, meeting unusual people, getting lost, stumbling across criminals in unlikely places, rescuing animals. They weren't going to do any of that in Glasgow. Holly would meet her mum, they'd have a bite of lunch and go round the shops together and then she'd get the train back. She'd make sure she caught the 4.30.

'Go for it!' cried Sylvie.

Holly rushed through to the bedroom, changed her top, brushed her hair, tied it back into its ponytail, grabbed her bag and was off, taking two stairs at a time on her way down. There wasn't much time to spare if she was going to catch the two o'clock train.

She leapt onto a bus just before the driver was about to close the door.

'Don't try that again,' he warned. 'You could get yourself killed.'

'Your dad would go his dinger if he knew what you were up to,' said Sylvie gleefully, as if she were enjoying the prospect.

Holly didn't wish to think about her dad. She made it to Waverley Station with ten minutes to go, just enough time to buy a ticket and find the platform. She had to run. The Glasgow train was already coming in.

'Maybe you should have left a note for your dad in case he did happen to come back early,' said Sylvie.

Too late for that now! Holly comforted herself with the thought that her dad never came home before his usual time.

The train arrived in Glasgow a couple of minutes early. Holly dodged through the crowds, put her ticket in the slot and went through the barrier. She paused for breath and scanned the crowds. No sign of her mum, not yet.

'She never is dead on time,' Sylvie reminded her.

In spite of knowing that, Holly was on edge. She couldn't help it. She felt anxious in stations, particularly on her own. It reminded her of the time when she was waiting for her dad to turn up in Edinburgh and he hadn't. It had not been his fault. Her mum just hadn't read his message telling her that he'd be back on leave from the Middle East a fortnight later than expected. Those were the two weeks she'd stayed with the Nightingales. If it hadn't been for Nina, Holly didn't like to think what might have happened to her.

Surely Mum wasn't going to let Holly down today? She'd sounded as excited as Holly was by the thought a shopping trip. Holly kept her eye on the long arms of the station clock as they moved slowly on, minute by minute. Five went by, then ten. She didn't want to watch them but somehow her eyes kept being drawn back.

'Have you got your mobile on you?' asked Sylvie.

Holly pulled open the drawstrings of her bag and rummaged through its jumbled contents, hairbrushes, combs, books, pens, coins. She began to unpack it. Then she began to panic. Where was the phone?

'You need to clean that out,' said Sylvie.

'Oh, shut up!' Holly snapped out loud and a man standing nearby gave her a funny look and shook his head.

'Can't you find it?' asked Sylvie.

'No!'

'Idiot! You know your dad told you to always keep your mobile with you at all times.'

She'd been in such a rush to catch the train that Holly hadn't had time to think about it. Her phone definitely wasn't in her bag. Holly felt quite sick.

She could have used a public telephone in the station if she'd known her mum's mobile number. But she didn't. People didn't keep mobile numbers in their heads. And Mum didn't have a landline telephone any more. She'd got cut off for not paying her bills on time.

It was now a quarter past three and they had been waiting for a full thirty minutes. It felt more like an hour.

A woman stopped to ask if Holly was all right. 'You look a bit lost?'

'I'm fine, thanks. I'm just waiting on my mum. I expect she'll be here soon.'

'I hope so, dear.' The woman walked off but gave Holly a backward look as if to make sure she was really all right.

And then Holly heard her mum's voice.

'Holly! Holly, love! I'm here.'

Holly turned and ran towards her mum, who was teetering along on her ridiculously high heels. She was waving madly.

They collided, laughing.

'Sorry I'm a bit late, hen.'

There was a bit of Holly that wanted to shout at her mum, demand to know why she'd kept her waiting. But she didn't want to waste another moment of their precious afternoon together.

'That's all right, Mum.'

'Listen, love, we'll need to go back to the flat before we head for the shops. I left my credit card on the kitchen table. Only minded it when I was on the bus.'

'But, Mum,' wailed Holly, 'I haven't had any lunch. I'm starving. And we don't have that much time. Remember I've got to catch the 4.30?'

Sharon shrugged. 'Come on to the cafe then. The one by the bus station. I've enough in my purse to buy you a sandwich.'

Holly chose a cheese and tomato roll and a glass of orange juice while Sharon had a cup of coffee. They ate at the outside tables. It wasn't much of a lunch but it was OK for Holly. She was happy just to be sitting beside her mum again and listening to her chatting about this and that – something she'd seen in the street that had made her laugh, a woman she'd got talking to on the bus. Sharon could make a story out of anything. She talked breathlessly. She always gave off a buzz of excitement as if she didn't have quite enough time to do all the things she wanted to do.

'That was great last night, pet, wasn't it? The two of us, talking about all those lovely faraway places. I think we'll go to Disney first. What do you say?'

'Don't hold your breath,' said Sylvie.

Holly ignored her. 'That'd be great, Mum.'

'I brought you a real nice bracelet back from Tenerife. I got it in the market. I have it up in the flat. I'll give it to you when we get home.'

Home. That no longer meant her mum's flat in Glasgow Holly realised.

'So, did your luggage come? Did you get it back from Lenny?' she asked.

Sharon seemed a bit flustered. 'Oh, aye, it turned up. This morning. Shall we go then, hen? We want to get to the shops before they shut.'

'Not much time left,' observed Sylvie, 'if you've to go to the flat first.'

It was nearly four now.

'Let's go!' cried Sharon.

They caught a bus quickly. Holly hadn't been in her old street since the day she left with her mum to catch the train to Edinburgh over three months ago. The crunched up feeling had returned to Holly's tummy, and it had nothing to do with the sandwich she'd just eaten. She wasn't supposed to go to the flat at all, the Social Services had made that plain. It was because of Lenny the Lion, Holly knew that, though they had not actually said so to her. He had a criminal record – for minor offences, according to her mum, breach of the peace, being in possession of a small quantity of drugs. He wasn't a dealer, Sharon had assured Holly. Not that Holly knew exactly what the difference was. He'd not been caught at least, said Dad.

As they neared Sharon's door her neighbour, Mrs Blackie, popped out of hers. She was the horror of the street, much worse than their Mrs McGinty in Edinburgh, who, Holly's dad said, was 'all mouth'. Mrs McGinty was a lonely woman who had nothing else to do all day, whereas Mrs Blackie caused trouble every chance she got. She was always on the lookout for things to report. Dogs fouling the pavement, folk dropping litter. Anything. The police got fed up with her. They'd told her off one day, said she was wasting their time and that was an offence she could be charged with. It didn't stop her, though. Sharon always said it had been Mrs Blackie who had clyped on Lenny about the drugs.

'Don't let her bother you, hen,' said Sharon, taking Holly's hand and heading up the path. 'She's just an old cow.'

'Don't tell me they've let you have her back to stay?' said Mrs Blackie, staring hard at Holly.

'Mind your own business,' snapped Sharon, not even breaking her stride. 'Ye'll get yer neb caught in the door one of these days.'

Holly giggled. That would be a good picture to draw: Mrs Blackie's nose trapped in the door.

She followed her mum up the stairs. They were just as they had always been, smelling of cat, needing a good clean. Not many here took their turns of washing the stair and sometimes Sharon would get so fed up she'd lose her temper and go up and down the stairs slopping water at a great rate, making as much noise as she could so that people opened their doors and poked their heads out to see what was going on. She usually left a flood in the bottom passage.

She unlocked the door of the flat and they went in.

Lolling at the kitchen table drinking a cup of tea, his reddish-gold hair swept back from his forehead like a lion's mane, was Lenny.

Nine

'Hiya, how ya doin', Doll?' said Lenny, winking at Holly.

She didn't answer. She was too shocked.

'Long time no see. Course you're not allowed to come visiting the Big Bad Wolf, are you?' He laughed and made a growling sound.

'Thinks he's funny,' said Sylvie.

'Oh, shut up, Lenny,' snapped Sharon. She was clearly thrown by the sight of him. 'And her name's Holly.'

'Near enough. Holly. Dolly.'

'Didn't expect to see you here,' said Sharon, giving him a hard stare.

'Finished my business early.'

Holly wondered what kind of business that might be.

'Best not to know,' advised Sylvie.

Lenny winked again at Holly. 'You're getting tall. And bonny with it. You used to be just a wee squit.'

'She's shooting up right enough,' said Sharon. She sounded nervous. 'I've just come in for my credit card. I want to take Holly shopping.'

'Got any credit on it?' asked Lenny. 'We tried it last day in Tenerife, remember?'

'Yes, so we did. I'd forgotten.' Sharon bit her lip. 'Maybe the machine in the shop wasne working properly.'

'Those machines are always working. I could let you

have a couple of twenties.' Lenny dug in his pocket and pulled out a thick wad of notes. Holly had never seen so many, not all at one time. Her dad took three or four at a time out of the hole-in-the-wall. 'Had a win on the dogs,' Lenny added.

'We don't need to go shopping, Mum,' said Holly quickly. Time was moving on. She'd have to start making a move back to Edinburgh soon. Her dad would go spare if he came in from work and found her missing. And he'd go berserk if he thought she was in Mum's flat in Glasgow with Lenny here, offering to give her money.

'There you are, Shar,' said Lenny, slapping down one, two, three, twenty-pound notes on the table. 'Be my guest. Get yourself something nice. I like to treat people, don't I, Shar?'

Holly's mum didn't answer but she gathered up the notes as fast as she could and stuck them in her pocket.

'And this one is especially for you, Hol.' Lenny held out another twenty pound note.

'It's all right, thanks.' Holly backed away.

'Oh, come on! You not allowed to touch my money, is that it? Too dirty for you?'

'I don't need it.'

'Everybody needs money.'

'Leave it, Lenny,' said Sharon.

'Dad rolling in money, is he then, Hol?' said Lenny, brushing off Sharon's hand from his shoulder.

'I said leave it, Lenny,' repeated Sharon. She was getting angry.

A mobile rang on the shelf and Sharon went to get it,

but Lenny tilted his chair backwards and reached it first.

'Sharon Anderson residence. Who's speaking, please?' He grinned and nodded. 'Oh, it's Holly's dad, is it?'

'No!' shrieked Sharon, covering her face with her hands.

Holly took a step towards her mother. What was her dad doing home so early?

Lenny put on a phoney voice. 'How nice to speak to you, Joe. Yes, it's Lenny here. And what can I do for you?'

Holly could imagine only too well what her dad would be saying.

'Have I seen your daughter? Well, that *is* an interesting question. Very interesting.'

'Hope he doesn't have a heart attack when he finds out you're here,' said Sylvie.

This was definitely one of the times when Holly wished Sylvie would keep her thoughts to herself.

'Give me that, Lenny! Let me speak to him!' Sharon tried to grab the mobile but Lenny turned so it was out of her reach.

'Let me just exchange a few civil words with your ex,' he said, as if it was the most reasonable thing in the world

'Give it to me!' shouted Sharon. She was panicking now.

Suddenly Holly stepped up to Lenny. 'I want to speak to my dad,' she said, glaring at him.

'You seem popular, Joe,' said Lenny. 'You've no idea. They're both trying to grab the phone from me. Yes, your daughter is here too. Is that why you're phoning? Pretty little thing – taking after her mum.'

Holly could hear the boom of her dad's voice at the end of the line. She couldn't make out what he was saying exactly but she didn't need to.

'All right, all right, keep your hair on, Joe,' said Lenny eventually. He took the phone away from his ear and turned back to Holly and her mum. 'Calm down, you two. You're like a couple of harpies. Which one do you want to speak to first, Joe? Sharon? OK. Nice talking to you, Joseph.' He held out the phone to Sharon.

Holly's mum had to listen to a tirade before she was allowed to get a word in. Meanwhile Lenny whistled softly to himself, leaning backwards in the chair, with his hands linked behind his head.

'But, Joe,' said Sharon, once she was permitted to speak, 'Holly was lonely all on her own so I thought there would be no harm in her coming to Glasgow for a couple of hours. I was going to take her shopping. I didn't know Lenny was going to be in. Honest I didn't. I wouldn't have brought Holly here if I had.'

Lenny laughed. He was loving this. 'Lenny the Big Bad Wolf?' he whispered to Holly, showing his teeth. Then he started to sing, 'Who's afraid of the Big Bad Wolf.' Holly kept her expression stony. She didn't like him but she wasn't afraid of him. He'd never harmed her in any way. Nor her mother, as far as she knew, and her mum told her most things. Sharon was no good at keeping secrets.

'I'm awfy sorry, Joe, if you were worried,' Sharon sounded beaten now. 'But there's no need to get onto the Social Services. She wasn't in any harm.'

Lenny gave up singing and went back to whistling softly.

'OK, so I know I'm not supposed to bring her here,' Sharon carried on, her voice rising. 'It was an emergency. I'd no money on me. What was I to do? I'd promised Holly I'd take her shopping. I couldn't let her down.' She turned to Holly. 'He wants to speak to you, love.'

Holly took the mobile and turned her back on her mum and Lenny. 'Dad? It's me, Holly. I'm sorry.'

At that point the mobile went dead.

Holly looked at the display in horror. 'No battery,' she said. She'd wanted to talk to Dad and try to smooth things over.

'Oh, no,' groaned Sharon. 'I haven't charged it since I came back. Everything's goin' up the spout today.'

'You said it, Shar,' said Lenny.

'Just shut up!' Sharon covered her face with her hands.

'You can use my mobile if you want, Shar,' offered Lenny in a low voice. 'That's if you're sure you won't catch some terrible disease from it.' He laid it on the table.

Sharon picked it up. 'Do you know your dad's mobile number, Holly?'

'No, but you can phone the landline.'

Sharon dialled the Edinburgh number. 'It's engaged. Who's he phoning now? This is gettin' out of hand.'

'That's life,' said Lenny.

Sharon made a face at him.

'Hope he's not ringing the Social Services. Then you really will be in the schmuck.' Lenny sounded not displeased.

'Try again, Mum,' urged Holly. She was desperate to talk to her dad, to explain to him. Her mum rubbed him up the wrong way, but Holly might have more luck. She didn't want the Social Services involved either, not if it meant she'd see even less of her mum.

Sharon, who by now was looking thoroughly flustered, got through on the fourth try. 'Joe,' she began, but got no further. She listened for a moment before carrying on. 'All right, all right, don't go on! I'll take Holly to the station this very minute and bring her back on the train to Edinburgh. I'll come with her myself. No, I won't just leave her with a stranger – that's uncalled for, Joe.' She was cut off again by Holly's dad. When there was a pause she said, 'Holly, your dad wants to speak to you.'

'I'm sorry, Dad,' Holly began but got no further then, either.

'Now look, Holly,' he said, 'listen carefully. Sharon will take you down to Queen Street Station straightaway. I want you out of that flat!' He was almost shouting. She had never heard him so upset. 'You understand?'

'Yes, Dad.' Get away from Lenny in particular, he meant.

'You are to wait with your mother at the outdoor cafe and stay put until I come for you. And you are not under any circumstances to move one millimetre from there. Understand?' he asked again.

'Yes, Dad.' She wanted to ask if she was in trouble, but not with Lenny listening.

'I'll speak to your mother again now.'

He must have given Sharon the same instructions.

'Sorry about the shopping, love,' sighed Sharon once he'd rung off. 'I wanted to get you something nice. I'll do it next time I come through to Edinburgh.'

'Your old man was really going his dinger, Hol,' said Lenny happily.

Holly didn't answer.

'We'll be off then, Lenny,' said Sharon, seizing her bag.

'Aye, you'd better. Before the polis come nosing around.'

As Holly and Sharon made a move towards the door Lenny's mobile rang.

'Is that Joe?' Sharon asked anxiously, but Lenny shook his head.

'Hi, Billy . . .' Lenny got no further. He sat bolt upright in his chair. 'You're kiddin' me on!'

'Let's go, pet,' said Sharon, shoving Holly towards the door.

'No, wait!' Lenny held up his hand like a policeman stopping the traffic. He listened carefully. 'A tip-off, you say? Who do you think – ? No!' He swore.

'Bad news?' asked Sharon, as nervous as a kitten.

'OK, OK!' Lenny was standing now. He was frowning and running his fingers through his hair. 'Don't worry. I'll see to that right now.' He finished the call.

'What's wrong, Lenny?' asked Sharon.

'Hang on a minute.' He dashed off into the bedroom. They heard him opening a drawer. 'I need you to help me with something . . .' he called.

'Relax, pet,' Sharon said to Holly. 'We've plenty time. It'll take your dad a good hour or more to get here from

Edinburgh. He hasnae got wings, and just as well.'

Lenny returned carrying a small package wrapped in brown paper. 'Shar, do me a favour, eh?' His tone had changed and Holly recognised the voice he used when he wanted to be in her mum's good books. Lenny the Lion's roar had turned to a purr. 'Put this in your bag and drop it off at Jacko's for me. You can do it after you've been to the station. You know where Jacko hangs out, don't you?'

'Yes, but –' Sharon began.

'Do it, Shar, *please*!' He laid the package on the table. 'I'm not asking much.'

'I've told you before I don't want anything to do with –'

'It's nothing like the last time, honestly! Just do it, if you don't we'll be for it, good and proper, you and me. They could be here any minute.'

'The polis?' Sharon practically shrieked the word.

Lenny ignored her and turned to Holly. 'Just forget you've seen or heard anything. Understand?'

Holly nodded. All she'd seen was a package. And the panic in his eyes.

'If you blab you'll get me and your mum in trouble. Deep trouble,' he stressed. 'You wouldn't want to hurt your mum, would you?'

Ten

'Don't go on at her, Lenny,' said Sharon. 'She's a smart kid. I know she'll keep her lip buttoned.'

'She'd better!'

Lenny fished in his pocket and pulled out the stack of notes.

'Here, take these, kid, and put them in the bottom of your bag. Buy yourself something in Edinburgh. And not a word to your dad. Right?'

He thrust the notes into Holly's palm. She could almost feel the money burning her hand. She didn't want to take it but she had to. She stared at the bank notes, lying there in the palm of her hand. She curled her fingers round them and shoved them right down into the bottom of her bag, as Lenny had instructed. Then she pulled the drawstrings tightly together.

Sharon was staring at the package on the table. She still hadn't touched it.

Lenny picked it up and faced her. 'You've got to do this for me, Sharon.'

'Put it in another bag or something, Lenny!'

'It won't bite you. Just take it, will you?'

Holly had never seen him like this.

'Cover it up first! It looks –' Sharon broke off.

Looks what? Holly wondered. Why was her mum so

scared of it? It looked very ordinary and harmless to her. But why wouldn't Lenny explain what it contained?

'You know why,' Sylvie said, but Holly wasn't about to listen.

Lenny swore again.

'Not in front of Holly, Lenny,' said Sharon. 'Mind your language! I've told you before.'

'All right, all right! I'll find a bag.' Lenny glanced round the room and spotted an orange supermarket carrier bag in the corner. He upended it and oranges and apples rolled in all directions across the floor. Holly went scrambling after them.

'Leave them!' shouted Lenny so loudly that Holly backed off. He'd never behaved like this before. 'You've got to get out of here, the two of you. Fast!'

He slid the packet into the supermarket bag and swung it over to Sharon. 'Now put that in your bag! You've enough rubbish in there to hide it under. And don't waste any more time. Just go, Sharon! Go!'

'But what about you, Lenny?'

'I'll be all right. Place is clean, isn't it? Clean as a whistle.'

Holly suddenly wondered where that phrase came from. Were whistles *that* clean? She must ask Nina.

But she'd seen enough crime series on the telly to know exactly what Lenny was talking about. It meant that there was no incriminating evidence in the flat. It was in Mum's bag now.

'It's better I stay,' Lenny went on. He was sounding calmer now. Now that he'd done what had to be done. 'If

I'm not here they'll break the door down. Anyway, shows I've nothing to hide.' He held his arms out wide. His old familiar smile was back

'But what about Mum?' Holly protested. 'She'll get into trouble!'

'Go!' snapped Lenny. The smile had disappeared again. He thrust his face close to Holly's. 'Scarper!'

Sharon seized Holly by the hand and yanked her out of the flat. The door slammed shut behind them. They ran down the stairs as fast as Sharon's heels would allow. On the last step she went over on her ankle but Holly held on to her and she managed to right herself.

Mrs Blackie was still hanging around her doorway as they went out.

'Short visit, Holly,' she commented. 'Long enough, I dare say.'

Sharon and Holly walked rapidly on.

Halfway along the street they bumped into Norma, Sharon's neighbour and best friend, who lived across the landing. When Holly had been living with her mum she'd seen a lot of Norma.

'Holly!' Norma dropped her bulging shopping bags to give her a hug. 'Great to see you, pal. I miss you. How are you doin'?' Norma was all set for a good blether. 'Are you takin' to Edinburgh? Not as good as Glasgae, eh?' She laughed.

'It's all right,' said Holly.

Sharon was glancing nervously up and down the street. 'Norma,' she said abruptly, 'we cannae stop, I'm afraid. Holly's a train to catch.'

'Oh, OK.' Norma sounded disappointed. 'I'll come through and see you in Edinburgh sometime, will I, Holly?'

'That'd be nice.'

'I fancy a day out in Edinburgh.'

'See you, Norma,' said Sharon. 'We've really got to run. Catch you up later.'

And run they did, though for Sharon it was more of a hobble.

As they reached the main road they saw a black taxi coming round the corner. Sharon stepped into the middle of the road and waved it down. They scrambled aboard and Sharon slammed the door shut just as a police car turned into the street with its blue lights flashing and its siren wailing.

'Queen Street Station.' Sharon lent forward to speak to the driver. 'We're in a hurry!'

'I'll see what I can do, hen.'

A second police car came into view.

'Wonder what's goin' on along there,' said the driver, but he pulled sharply away from the kerb and said no more. Sharon leaned back and heaved a sigh of relief. Holly hung onto the strap. They hadn't even had time to fasten their seat belts. The driver was taking Sharon at her word, hurtling along side streets, overtaking cars and shooting the lights. Holly tried to buckle her belt but her fingers fumbled and couldn't find the slot. On her lap sat her bag containing Lenny's dirty notes. And on the floor between Sharon's feet rested her bag with Lenny's package inside. Holly couldn't take her eyes off it.

'That was a near one,' said Sharon, to herself more than to Holly.

'Here we are then, ladies,' said the driver as he wheeled sharply into Queen Street Station, sending them flying across the back seat. 'You OK there?'

'Fine,' said Sharon, groping for her purse. Of course it was empty, so she turned to Holly.

'Give us one of those notes,' she whispered, pointing to Holly's bag.

Holly rummaged around until she found the bundle, and passed them to her mother who paid the driver, giving him a good tip.

'Thanks, hen,' he said. 'Hope you make your train.'

Now that they were at the station, and there was a bit of time to spare, Sharon cheered up. 'I think we're needing a cup of tea,' she said. 'Want something else to eat, pet?'

Holly shook her head. 'Not hungry.' The bumpy ride had made her feel queasy.

They found a couple of seats at an empty table. It was loaded with dirty cups and plates but a young man soon came to clear it up.

'I've seen you somewhere,' he said to Sharon. 'Where do you work?'

Sharon beamed. 'The *Spike*. The *Silver Spike*.'

'That's where I've seen you! Just been a couple of times. Great place. Must go again soon.'

He wanted a chat but suddenly Sharon was in no mood for it. She kept looking over her shoulder. She wouldn't want Dad to see her being chatted up, thought

Holly. What was it with her parents at the moment? It seemed everyone they met was a potential girlfriend or boyfriend. Eventually the man shrugged and gave up, piled up the dishes and moved on.

'Holly,' said Sharon, bringing her chair closer, 'not a word about any of this, eh, to anybody?'

Holly nodded. The truth was that she didn't know what she would tell anybody – she had her suspicions, but she was still pretty baffled by what had gone on back in the flat.

'Lenny's just got himself into a wee bit of trouble,' said Sharon. 'Nothing big, you understand.'

'It's OK, Mum.' Couldn't she just leave it? They only had a few more minutes before Dad would arrive and take her home. Holly wished things could be normal with Mum, but there was always some drama or other.

'I'm sorry about this, love. Wait till I see him later! He shouldn't be asking me –' Sharon broke off and said no more, sipping her tea. 'And me with my work to go to.' She glanced at her watch.

'I didn't realise you were working tonight. Will you be all right, Mum?' asked Holly. 'For time?'

Her mum would have to go home and change and be at the *Silver Spike* by nine. And before that she'd have to take the package to Jacko. Whoever he was, *wherever* he was. Why couldn't Lenny do his own deliveries?

'Best we don't know,' said Sylvie.

'I'll manage,' said Sharon, opening up her bag.

'Careful, Mum,' whispered Holly.

'It's all right, Hol. I'll just do my face while we're

waiting. Don't worry, love. I won't leave you. Not till your dad turns up.'

She dared not, Holly was aware of that. It sounded as if Dad wouldn't be offering her any more chances.

Sharon put the bag between her feet and began to rummage amongst the contents. 'It would have to be at the very bottom!' She pulled out her make-up bag and all sorts of odds and ends came tumbling out. Hair brushes, packets of tissues. Lipsticks. *How many lipsticks did one person need*, wondered Holly.

Holly bent down to help pick them up. One of them rolled off and ended up under the next table. She went diving after it.

'Never mind that,' said Sharon. 'I've plenty others.'

The bag repacked, Sharon opened up a compact mirror and began to put on her eye make-up.

Holly kept a look out for Dad. Eventually his train arrived and he came striding through the barrier ahead of all the other passengers.

'Here he is!' She was both pleased and worried about seeing him.

'He's still all steamed up,' muttered Sharon. 'You can see that a mile off.'

She succeeded in getting the first word in though. Holding her hand palm out in front of herself, she said, 'Look, Joe, I'm dead sorry, it was just that we hadn't realised the time. Holly should have gone back to Edinburgh on the four thirty. She'd have been back in good time.'

Dad put his hand on Holly's shoulder. 'But she wasn't.

You never realise the time, Sharon. Ever since I've known you . . . One day you'll go too far.'

Holly could see that he was still very upset. 'I'm fine, though, Dad . . .' she began.

'We only went to the flat to get some money –'

'I don't care what it was for. Holly shouldn't have come through to Glasgow in the first place and she knows that.' His expression let Holly know they'd be having words later.

'I'm sorry, Dad,' she put in. 'I shouldn't have come. It's all my fault.'

'No, it is not. You're the child. She's the adult. This mustn't ever happen again, Sharon.'

'That sounds like a threat.' Sharon stood up and put her hands on her hips.

'Take it whatever way you want. But you know perfectly well that Holly is not allowed to go to your flat under any circumstances. Especially with that . . .' He stopped and pushed his fingers through his hair. 'I think you and I should have a word, Sharon. Holly, stay put, will you?' He moved a few steps away, indicating that Sharon should follow.

Holly shifted about on her seat. She couldn't wait to get home now – she'd had a late night with Mum the previous evening, and she was weary. But Dad seemed to have quite a bit he wanted to say. While Holly was waiting for them to finish their discussion she happened to glance down and saw, underneath the chair Sharon had been sitting on, the plastic supermarket bag with Lenny's package inside it. Holly looked around, horrified. What if somebody else had seen it? Lying there for anyone in the station to pick up. The place was milling with people. Two policemen walked past. Holly's heart raced.

'Calm down,' said Sylvie. 'They're just on patrol. They're not looking at you.'

Holly stared down at the packet again. It must have fallen out when Sharon had been looking for her make-up.

Holly glanced around. She couldn't just leave it lying there. What if her dad noticed it when he came back? He might pick it up – anyone could pick it up. She might not know exactly what the package contained, but she doubted it was legal. People were going about their business, heading to and from the platforms, and no one was paying any attention to her, not that she could see. Her mum and dad had their backs to her with him doing most of the talking.

Holly leaned over sideways, letting her right arm slide under the table. She grasped the bag and in a second had it up on her lap. Nobody seemed to have noticed. Her face was burning.

'All right if I sweep under your table?'

Holly's head jerked round to see the man who'd been cleaning the table earlier. He was holding a brush now. Had he seen her pick up the package?

'If he did he wouldn't know what's in it,' said Sylvie.

'OK?' he asked again.

Holly nodded and lifted her feet out of the way.

'Folk can be right messy,' he commented. 'They'll drop anything.'

She was still clutching the package on her knee.

'Ta, love,' he said and then he moved on.

Panicking, Holly shoved the package into her bag and pulled the strings together.

Her dad and Sharon came back. Sharon's face looked flushed.

'We'll be on our way then, Holly,' said Dad.

Sharon glanced at the station clock. 'Jings, is that the time! I'll need to fly, Joe, or I'll be late.'

'Story of your life,' said Dad, but he was looking calmer now.

Sharon bent down and kissed Holly. 'See you next Sunday, hen. Usual time. Look forward to it. We'll have a great day. Bye, Joe. Awfy sorry again for your trouble.' And with that she flew.

Dad stood there, watching, shaking his head. He sighed. 'Sharon'll never change. She's as dizzy as the day I met her – just like a teenager.'

'Maybe when she's forty?' suggested Holly.

She'd made her dad laugh at least.

'Come on, then, love.' He held out his hand. 'We'll just make the next train if we run.'

Eleven

All the way home in the train Holly could think of one thing only. The package. What was she to do with it? She felt as edgy as if she were carrying a stick of dynamite.

'It can't blow up,' said Sylvie. 'At least that's one thing you don't have to worry about.'

Holly's dad was in no mood to talk. He sat with his arms folded across his chest, staring straight ahead.

They took a taxi from the station. When they got out he said they'd need to get something to eat and they stopped to fetch carry-out pizza. Dad said something about cooking a proper meal the next day, but little else. He was very tense.

They carried their pizzas up the stairs. In spite of worrying herself sick about what was going on with her Mum, Holly found she was starving. She hadn't eaten much all day and it was now gone nine o'clock.

As they passed Anna's door Cindy gave a low bark. The door opened.

'Sorry about that,' said Anna, holding the dog's collar. 'I've got a parcel here for you, Joe. A delivery. I took it in.'

'That was kind of you.'

'No problem. Come on in.'

They went inside, with Dad carrying their pizza boxes aloft. Cindy did a little dance of welcome around them and ran up and down the hall with a slipper in her mouth.

'That's to show she regards you as a friend,' said Anna to Holly.

Holly crouched down to stroke the dog and took a look around. There were pictures all around the pale green walls and the floor runner was dark green. A vase of roses stood on the side table. The flat felt and smelled nice, Holly thought, not drab like theirs. She must get her dad to help her decorate her room. And the rest of the place too.

Anna lifted a box from a side table in the hall and passed it to Holly's dad.

'These'll be my new binoculars.' He set down the pizza boxes and lifted the parcel.

'Do you go birdwatching?' asked Anna.

'Don't tell me,' said Sylvie, 'she's a birdwatcher too!'

'I do, as a matter of fact,' said Joe, a bit sheepishly. He unwrapped his parcel and took out a pair of brand new binoculars. 'Fantastic!' He held them to his eyes though he can't have been able to see anything except the other end of the hall.

'So do I!' exclaimed Anna. 'I love birdwatching when I have the chance. Where do you usually go?'

'I like the John Muir Trust down at Dunbar, on the coast.'

'So do I!' exclaimed Anna again.

'I knew she'd say that,' said Sylvie, smugly.

Holly hoped they weren't going to spend too long chatting. The pizzas would be going cold. And she was desperate to get rid of the package.

'Where do you think you're going to put it?' asked Sylvie, while Anna and Dad discussed the finer points of some rare seabird that had been reported in the news recently. 'No idea, have you?'

Holly hadn't.

Anna and Dad carried on blethering. At least her dad was looking a bit more relaxed now.

'Well, I'd love to go with you, next time you're heading down to Dunbar,' Anna was saying.

'It'll be a Sunday,' said Dad. 'Holly's with her mum on a Sunday.'

'Suits me,' said Anna.

She and Dad smiled briefly at each other and then he put the binoculars back in their box.

'Sorry, dear. I know, you must be starving. We haven't eaten,' he explained to Anna. 'We've been in Glasgow.'

'To see my mum,' Holly put in. 'But she wasn't able to come back with us tonight.'

Her dad gave her an odd look but said nothing. 'Come on then, love,' he said. 'And thanks again, Anna.'

'Pleasure. See you Sunday? Let's see what the weather's like.'

By the time Holly and her dad got upstairs the pizzas were stone cold and floppy but Dad was definitely in a better mood.

'It's all right,' he said. 'I'll put the oven on and we can heat them up. Have a banana while you're waiting.' He must have been to the supermarket at lunchtime because the fruit bowl was full.

It would take fifteen minutes to heat the oven and another fifteen to bring the pizzas back to life. She had thirty minutes to work out what to do with Lenny's package.

Holly went into her room, closed the door and put her back to it. There was no question of telling Dad. He might call the police. And then Mum could be arrested and locked up in jail. It was possible, wasn't it? That's what happened on the telly, but Holly didn't know for sure. She just felt terrified by the idea of it. She'd have to hide the stuff for now, until she decided how best to get rid of it.

Holly's stomach began to churn as she tipped the contents of her bag onto her bed and saw Lenny's package.

'I suppose you could flush it down the toilet after tea, but you'd have to take it out its wrapper to do that and you might get the stuff all over you.' Sylvie said.

Whatever the stuff was. It might be powder, Holly supposed, or tablets. But one thing she and Sylvie were agreed on was that it must be drugs of some kind. Illegal drugs. They'd had talks about such things at school from a policeman once.

'Holly,' said her dad, opening the door a crack, 'would you like extra cheese on your pizza?'

She shoved the carrier bag under the bed. Her heart was racing.

'Would you?' repeated her dad, pushing the door a little wider.

'Oh yes, yes please!' She went and opened the door, not wanting to keep him waiting.

'Are you all right? You're looking a bit flushed. You're not running a temperature, are you?'

'No, I'm fine, Dad. A wee bit tired.'

He laid the palm of his hand on her forehead. 'You feel a bit hot.'

'I'm fine. Really.'

He left her and went to put cheese on the pizzas.

'Whew!' said Sylvie. 'That was a near one.'

It wouldn't do to leave the bag under the bed. Dad might pull it out to vacuum the carpet. Every now and then he took a notion to vacuum the flat from end to end. He was house proud, was Dad.

'What about your bottom drawer?' suggested Sylvie, after a pause.

That was where Holly kept her winter sweaters and fleeces.

Holly tugged the drawer open. It tended to stick, especially when it was stuffed over-full, as it was at present. She eased the plastic bag in, sandwiching it between two of her thickest sweaters. That should be a safe enough place. She pushed the drawer back in. She had to give it an extra hard shove as it was sticking even more now.

'It can't stay in there for ever,' remarked Sylvie.

Holly didn't want to think about that. For now the stuff was out of sight. She went into the bathroom to wash her hands thoroughly, soaping them again and again.

'Your fingerprints will be on the bag of course,' said Sylvie. 'Bound to be.'

And Sharon's. And Lenny's.

'Holly,' called her dad. 'Coming?'

She went through to the kitchen.

'Pizzas are ready,' he said and they sat down to eat.

'What was Lenny up to while you were there?' he asked after they had munched their way through half of the pizza.

Holly shrugged. 'Nothing much.' She really didn't want to talk about that man with her dad.

'Does he have a job?'

'Not sure.'

Her dad let it go at that.

'The holidays are a problem,' he said. 'You at home alone, me at work. I don't like it but there's not much I can do about it.'

'I'm OK, Dad. Don't worry. I can go to Nina's a lot of the time.'

They didn't have any relatives Holly could go to. Her dad's mum and his brother lived in Leeds. He didn't often see or hear from them.

'Nina's very good to you,' he said.

'I know,' said Holly. If Nina hadn't been going to Perth today, she might never have found herself in this terrible predicament.

Once they'd eaten the pair of them began to get ready for bed.

After her dad had gone into the bathroom Holly noticed that the blue light was flashing on the telephone answering machine. She lifted the receiver. They had one new message. Perhaps it was Mum, wondering where the package was. She must have realised it was missing by now.

'Hello, Joe. It's Cerise. I'd really like to have a chat with you. Maybe you could call me back? I'll be in all evening.'

'Delete it!' urged Sylvie. 'Quickly.'

Holly deleted the message just as her dad was coming out of the bathroom. She still had her hand on the receiver.

'Any messages?'

'No.' Holly avoided his eye. 'I thought there might have been one from Mum, checking to see if we were home safe.'

Her dad shook his head. He knew, as Holly herself did, that her mum would never think of doing that. Sharon lived in the moment. She didn't look backwards or forwards.

'Doesn't mean she doesn't love you,' said Sylvie.

Holly knew that, too.

'Well,' sighed her dad, 'I think we've had enough excitement for one day. Don't know about you but I'm dead beat. On you go and get some sleep, love. And, Holly?'

Holly looked up warily.

'Don't put me through that again, OK? When there was no answer here and none on your mobile, I was beside myself with worry.'

'OK. Sorry, Dad.'

'I know, but I'd rather you'd no need to be.'

And that was the matter done. For now. Dad gave her a goodnight hug and they went to bed. Holly avoided looking at the bottom drawer. She didn't want to think about the package any more, not tonight at any rate, but in spite of feeling tired she found she couldn't get to sleep. She had too much boiling away inside her head. She listened to the traffic down in the street below. It wasn't as hectic as in the daytime but it was still quite steady. A siren wailed out into the night. Police or ambulance. Or a fire perhaps. There had been one in a shop across the street last week.

Sharon would be in the *Silver Spike*, chatting and laughing with the customers. She called herself a night bird. She hated mornings.

What had she done when she'd found the package was missing from her bag? Lenny would have gone berserk when she told him. She'd have had to tell him. And then there was Jacko. He wouldn't be too pleased either, presumably.

Holly wondered if her dad would be lying awake too. Maybe she should have told him about all of Cerise's phonecalls.

'But you don't want to have to put up with Cerise, do you?' said Sylvie. 'And Almondine?'

'What if he really is in love with her?'

'Don't be daft!' scoffed Sylvie. 'How could he be?'

Sylvie was right. Her dad was a sensible man. Nina had said so and she, being a writer, was a good judge of character. Or at least Holly hoped so. Although Nina seemed to think Holly was sensible too and look how that was turning out . . .

Everything was too much. Holly turned over and eventually went to sleep.

Twelve

When the phone rang in the morning Holly approached it cautiously. It could be any one of a number of people she didn't want to talk to. Cerise. Lenny. Mum, for she might ask whether Holly had seen the package if she'd found it was missing? But it was probably too early for her. Holly let the phone ring for a few seconds longer before lifting the receiver.

'Hi, is that you, Holly?'

It was an English voice, quite unlike her own Scottish one. She didn't recognise it.

Then the caller said, 'It's me, Lauren. I got your number from Nina. She said you might come over today, but that you might like a change. Mum and I are going for a run down the coast and to have a swim. Do you like swimming?'

'Yes. Oh yes, I do.'

'It's a gorgeous day. It's going to be hot.'

In the flat it was cool. The sun hadn't penetrated yet.

'Anyway,' Lauren went on, 'we were wondering if you'd like to join us? We're going to take a picnic. It'd be great if you could come with us.'

Holly didn't know what to say. She felt awkward – and quite flattered. She scarcely knew Lauren.

'She's not got any friends here yet, has she?' said Sylvie.

'That's why she's after you. But it might be good to get away from here and stop staring at that drawer.'

'Please do come!' urged Lauren.

'Thank you,' said Holly primly. 'I'd like to.'

'Oh, good! Bring your swimsuit. Mum thinks maybe she should have a word with your mum, just to make sure it's all right with her.'

Holly's heart sank. 'She's not here.'

'Does she work?'

'She's in Glasgow.'

Holly heard Anna talking to her mother in the background and then she came on again to say, 'What about your dad?'

'He's at work.'

'Oh, I see.'

She doesn't see anything, thought Holly.

Lauren relayed this information to her mother.

'Well, could you contact your dad then? Mum thinks he should know.'

After the chaos of yesterday Holly agreed. 'I can phone him on his mobile.'

'Great. We'll pick you up in half an hour or so. Just after ten?'

'I could come over to you. I know the way.'

'No, Mum says it'd be easier for us to pick you up on the way out of the city. Where do you live, exactly?'

Holly wished she'd thought up an excuse not to go but it was too late now. Their street was decidedly un-posh, compared to the Grange, the peaceful suburb where Lauren's family and the Nightingales lived, with its big houses and stone walls and beautiful trees overhanging the pavement. Holly and her dad lived in a grey stone tenement and the shops round about were a motley lot, as her dad put it, with cheap convenience stores, tattoo parlours, pubs, charity shops, Polish restaurants, Chinese and Indian carry-outs, and almost anything else you could think of. The truth was that Holly liked it. She loved to dawdle along looking in the windows. The Grange was a quiet area of the city. Leith Walk was not.

'Are you still there?' asked Lauren. 'Holly?'

'Yes.'

'So what's your address?'

Holly gave her the information and waited while Lauren wrote it down.

Having come recently to Edinburgh from London, Lauren, of course, had no idea where it was. 'But don't worry. We'll find you. Mum's got a satnav. What number?'

Reluctantly, Holly told her.

'Pick you up just after ten?'

'OK.'

Holly texted her dad on his mobile, which was easier for him to check if he was on the shop floor. He worked for an engineering firm run by one of his pals, an old school friend. Along with Cerise. They might all have been pals at school together, thick as thieves.

'Stop that!' ordered Sylvie. 'You're just annoying yourself and you know it. Get moving before they get here!'

That certainly made Holly shift. She went frantically through her drawers looking for her swimsuit, finding it eventually at the bottom of the dirty clothes basket where she'd dumped it after she'd been at the baths last time. She pressed it to her nose. It stank of chlorine.

'Oh no! I can't wear that!'

There was no choice, as Sylvie pointed out. And once Holly was in the sea the smell would go.

'Thing is not to go too close to them before you do.'

Holly wrapped the costume in a towel and squeezed it into a carrier bag. She couldn't find a bigger one. She wondered about taking her dad's sports bag but only for a second. It was brand new, a birthday present to himself, and he was proud of it. Holly hoped it might be a first step to going to the gym. Until recently he'd carried his kit in plastic bags.

She ran the iron over a pair of recently-washed shorts and a short-sleeved top. It was only when she'd put the top on that she realised there was a nasty stain right down the front. She tried rubbing it out with a wet cloth.

'That's not going to work,' commented Sylvie.

Holly yanked it off, found another and shoved it in the drier to smooth out the creases while she went to look for her flip-flops. They were too small, left over from last year, but she might need them on the beach.

'Slow down,' said Sylvie.

But Holly couldn't. She planned to be ready and waiting down in the street for Lauren and her mum before they got the chance to ring the bell. She didn't want them coming up the stairs. If they did, she'd have to ask them in.

She rescued the T-shirt from the drier and pulled it

on. It wasn't perfect but it would have to do. She was brushing her hair when the phone shrilled out in the hall. For a moment she thought of not answering but it might be Lauren again with some other instructions.

'Hi, Hol!' It was Johnny.

'Oh, hi.'

'When are you coming over? I've been waiting for you.'

'You mean this morning?'

'Of course.'

'I can't, Johnny.'

'What do you mean you can't?'

'Lauren – the girl next door to you –'

'I know who Lauren is,' he said impatiently. 'What's she got to do with it?'

'She's asked me to go to the beach with her and her mum.' The more Holly thought about it the less the trip appealed to her.

'But you said you were coming over here today.'

'No, I didn't.'

'Yes, you did. I was going to give you a tennis lesson.'

'But you didn't say it had to be today.'

'Yes, I did.'

'Well, I can't come, Johnny.' Holly was feeling downright miserable now. She would much rather spend the day with Johnny at his house than with people she hardly knew. Even if it meant playing tennis.

'Phone them up and say you've got flu.'

'Don't be daft. They'd see me in your garden.'

'So what?

'They'd know I was lying.'

'They'd be away before you got here.'

She wished he had rung half an hour earlier. 'Johnny, why don't you come with us? I'm sure they wouldn't mind.'

'Spend the day on the beach with Lauren's mum? You must be joking.'

Holly wished she was. 'Look, Johnny, I'll have to go. They could be here any minute and I've still to get ready.'

'Don't let me stop you. Hurry along now.' He was being sarcastic now.

'I'll see you tomorrow.'

'I'm busy tomorrow.' With that he put down the phone.

Holly didn't have time to ring him back to apologize; she felt even more miserable after Johnny's call. Why did things have to be so complicated? People things.

The door bell rang.

Thirteen

It was not the downstairs doorbell that had rung, but the one outside the door of the flat. So it couldn't be Lauren and her mum because the downstairs door was kept locked. It was likely to be Mrs McGinty with some kind of gripe.

But she was wrong. Holly opened the door to Lauren and her mother.

'A nice lady with a dog was coming out so she let us in,' explained Lauren's mum.

'Oh, erm, hello, Mrs . . .' Holly realised that she didn't even know Lauren's surname.

'Just Avril!' she said brightly. That didn't help. Avril was wearing what Holly believed were called Bermuda shorts, snow white, and an expensive looking black and white top. Beside her stood Lauren in blue and white candy-striped shorts with a blue top. They looked like some kind of magazine advert.

Holly had no option but to invite them in. She led them into the living room where she'd left her cereal bowl and mug sitting on the table. Her dad hadn't had time to wash his, either. They were piled up on the draining board beside a few other odds and ends.

'Sorry about the mess,' mumbled Holly, not looking in the direction of Lauren and her mum. Her face felt hot.

'That's all right, dear,' said Avril. 'Have you got your kit ready?'

'Almost. I'll not be a minute.'

'That's fine, we didn't give you much warning. Don't hurry, take your time. I'm going to have a look at the view from your window. It's wonderful!'

But Holly wanted to hurry and get them out of here as soon as possible. First of all she had to go to the loo. Then she cleaned her teeth and after that she went into the bedroom to check the contents of her bag. She pulled out the towel. It looked a bit ratty. Most of her dad's towels were old and growing threadbare. He kept saying he must buy some new ones. She found a dark green one in the linen cupboard. It didn't look too bad and she rammed it into the plastic bag, which looked ready to burst.

Before going back to the living room she took a quick look at herself in the mirror. A mistake. The T-shirt was a reddish-orange and didn't really suit her. She made a face at herself in the mirror. What must they think?

She found them standing at the living room window looking down on the street. It was particularly noisy that morning, or so it seemed to Holly. Four double-decker buses went past, one after the other in a convoy, and now an articulated lorry came rumbling down the road – heading for the port, probably. A police car screamed past.

Lauren and Avril turned round. They looked so neat and tidy that Holly gulped.

'Ready, dear?' asked Avril. 'Got everything? Your keys? You don't want to get locked out.'

Holly was grateful for the reminder, for she hadn't remembered her keys in the rush to get ready. Then, when they were about to go out the door, she realised that she hadn't switched off the iron and had to run back.

'Good thing you remembered that,' said Avril. 'You wouldn't want to burn the place down, would you?'

And to top it all off, Mrs McGinty was standing at her door, though that was only to be expected. She eyed Holly's visitors.

'Nice morning,' said Avril very politely.

Mrs McGinty grunted in reply. Perhaps Mrs McGinty had forgotten how to smile. Perhaps she'd had a lovely smile when she was younger. But Holly couldn't imagine Mrs McGinty as a girl. She waved to her as she hurried after Lauren and Avril, hoping the carrier bag wouldn't burst.

☆   ☆   ☆

The day, which had begun so badly, improved as it went on. They were heading for a beach quite far down the coast where Holly had never been, banked with sand dunes, apparently. So Lauren's mum said. Holly breathed a sigh of relief as they bypassed Portobello. At least there wouldn't be any chance of bumping into Almondine or Cerise where they were going.

When they arrived at the beach Holly and Lauren changed into their swimsuits straightaway and plunged into the sea, laughing as the cold water slapped against their legs. They raced each other into the waves. Holly was a strong swimmer like her dad. He had taught her to swim when she was small. She and Lauren swam a little too far out for Avril's liking and she called them back in.

The girls played with a beach ball, lay in the sun and chatted, swam again, and had a very nice picnic of ham and cheese baguettes, chipolata sausages, crisps and banana cake, along with Avril's homemade lemonade.

The only blip in the day came when Holly's mobile rang. It was her mum.

'Oh, hi, Mum.' Holly was wary. She moved away from Lauren and her mother, turning her back to them. Luckily the connection was bad and the sound of the waves was not helping.

'I can't hear you, Mum. I'm on the beach,' she shouted. 'With my friend Lauren, the one I told you about. Can I ring you back later?'

Holly could hear enough, however, to know that her mum was asking if she'd seen the supermarket bag, the one with the package for Jacko.

'I can't hear you, Mum,' Holly said. She couldn't think what else to say.

'I'll phone you later, love. I really need to talk to you.'

Holly did hear that. She went back to sit on the rug with Lauren and her mother.

'Everything OK?' asked Avril.

'Yes, fine, thank you.' She tried to forget Mum's call for the rest of the afternoon. Holly had learned some time ago it was better to put your worries in a box if you wanted to enjoy what was happening right at that moment. Though it wasn't always easy to do.

'I'm so pleased you were able to come with us today, Holly,' said Avril, as they were packing up to go home. She had passed the time sunbathing and reading a magazine. She was not at all like Nina.

The road back into town was busy but Holly arrived home before her dad, not that it mattered this time. He had got her text so he had known where she was. He was pleased she'd had a good day at the seaside.

'Seems you've got yourself a new pal.'

Holly nodded.

He cooked stir-fried chicken and noodles and Holly made a salad to go with it. They were finishing their meal when the phone rang.

Holly jumped up. 'I'll get it.'

It was not her mum, as she'd thought it might be.

'Is that you, Holly?' asked the caller.

Oh no . . . Holly was tempted to put the receiver down. But how could she do that, with her dad listening?

'Who is it, Holly?' he called.

'Cerise,' she told him reluctantly.

'She doesn't give up, does she?' said Sylvie.

Holly's dad came into the hall, took the receiver and went into his bedroom, closing the door behind him. Holly didn't dare eavesdrop, after what had happened last time. She couldn't tell by the expression on his face whether he was pleased to have taken the call or not.

She lay on her bed and tried to read but she couldn't concentrate. Her dad was on the phone for ages.

'Maybe not *ages*,' said Sylvie. 'Ten minutes.'

Soon it was fifteen.

'Stop counting!' said Sylvie.

'Shut up!' retorted Holly.

Finally, she heard her dad's door open. By then he had been talking to Cerise for getting on for half an hour.

He put his head round her door. 'Holly, love, I hope it's OK with you, but I'm popping out for a wee while?'

'With that woman!'

Dad frowned. 'Don't talk about her like that. That's very rude. She's got a name.'

'Cerise!' Holly knew she sounded childish, but she couldn't help it.

He ignored that and went on, 'I'm only going to see her for an hour to have a talk. I think I owe her that. I did walk out on her rather abruptly last weekend.' He was about to close the door, then he opened it again. 'Oh, by the way, you didn't tell me she'd phoned before.'

'I forgot,' muttered Holly.

He didn't believe her of course.

'You can get me on my mobile if you need to,' he said. He left.

Holly heard the front door closing. She turned on to her front and squashed her face into her pillow. She felt bad now.

'You could always ring in ten minutes time and tell him the kitchen's on fire,' suggested Sylvie.

After about half an hour, Holly became restless. She wandered up and down the hall and into the living room. She considered phoning Johnny, but he had put the phone down on her and she really felt it was up to him to make amends.

When the doorbell rang Holly ran to open it, telling herself that her dad had changed his mind, come back and found he'd forgotten his key. But her dad never did forget his key. He always slapped his hand against his pocket to make sure it was there.

Anna was standing on the landing, on her own for a change. There was no sign of Cindy.

'Holly, I was wondering if you and your dad would like to come down and have a meal with me one evening?'

Holly almost laughed out loud. Dad was having quite an effect on women these days. But she smiled instead. 'Oh – yes, thanks, I expect we would. Dad's gone out for a few minutes. Do you want to come in and wait for him?'

'Thank you, that would be lovely,' said Anna and she stepped inside.

Holly took her into the living room. It was not much tidier than it had been in the morning, but Anna didn't seem to notice and Holly didn't feel so uneasy about it, either. She asked what Holly had been doing all day and Holly told her about Lauren and the beach and swimming.

'How nice. It's good that you've made a new friend.'

They talked a while but there was still no sign of Holly's dad.

'He must have been away for over an hour,' observed Sylvie. 'Not like him to be late back.'

'You must feel a bit lonely at times all on your own, Holly,' said Anna.

'Dad's often at home in the evenings. It's usually fine.'

'Has he gone to meet a friend?'

Anna certainly didn't beat about the bush, did she? Well, nor would Holly. 'It's this woman! She's called Cerise.' Holly suddenly found herself pouring out the whole story of her dad and Cerise and Almondine, or as much as she knew of it. There were bits missing. Bits her dad must have kept to himself.

'Do you think he –' Anna hesitated, '– he is rather fond of Cerise?'

'Don't know how anyone could be! She's really horrible, Anna, honest she is. She made us stand on newspapers so that we wouldn't drip on her kitchen floor.'

'I suppose I can understand her point.' But Anna's expression suggested she understood Holly's point too.

'You wouldn't do that, would you?'

'Probably not. But some people are fussier than others. Doesn't mean they're *bad* . . .' Anna wrinkled her nose and Holly giggled.

When they heard the front door open they both fell silent, like conspirators.

'Holly?' called her dad.

'In here,' she called back.

'Sorry I've been a bit longer than I expected, love,' he said as he came into the room. He stopped dead when he saw Anna.

She sprang up. 'I was just going, Joe.'

'Anna wants us to come for a meal one evening, Dad,' said Holly quickly.

'Only if you feel like it,' put in Anna. 'You can let me know.'

'You don't have to go,' said Joe. He looked pleased to see her, now that he'd got over the surprise.

'No, I must. I have to take Cindy out for her evening walk. I'll see myself out.' She was gone before Joe could object.

He sat down on the settee.

'Cerise sends her regards, Holly. She says Almondine would love to see you.'

'Can he really and truly, cross his heart, believe that?' said Sylvie.

Holly said nothing.

'I suppose you wouldn't want to see her?' asked her dad.

'Why did he ask you if he knows that already?' asked Sylvie. 'He's all mixed up in his head if you ask me.'

So was Holly. She wished Cerise would go and jump into the sea at Portobello. At a deep part. And Lenny. Yes, Lenny too. He could jump into the river Clyde in Glasgow.

'Are you going to see her again, Dad?' asked Holly.

'Almondine?'

'No, Cerise.'

'I don't know, Holly. I just don't know. Perhaps. We've known each other a long time.'

They were silent for a moment, then Holly asked, 'What about Anna, Dad?'

'What about her?'

'She's asked us for a meal. Do you want to go?'

'Oh yes, I think we should. We can't very well refuse.'

'But would you like to?'

'What?'

'Refuse?' Really, he didn't seem to be all there.

'No, I wouldn't. I wouldn't dream of refusing. She's a nice woman. Don't you think?'

'Nicer than Cerise?'

'Well, obviously!' said Sylvie and Holly had to agree.

Dad shook his head. 'Holly, would you just shut up about Cerise.' He stood up and made a face at her – half cross, half not. 'It's none of your business.'

But it was, wasn't it? What if he did try to work things out with Cerise? It would turn Holly's life upside down yet again. And just when she was beginning to get used to living with Dad in Edinburgh. Mind you, if they moved out of this flat she could leave that chest of drawers behind. Dad was always promising to buy her a new one when they moved. But move in with Cerise? Surely not!

She didn't know which way to turn. When she went into her room she kicked out angrily at the bottom drawer – and stubbed her toe.

Fourteen

What *could* Holly do about Cerise? About any of the things that were nagging away at her?

She obviously couldn't talk about the package in her bottom drawer, but Holly brought up the subject of Cerise with Johnny the next morning. Holly had worried for half the night about falling out with him the day before, but he'd rung her as if nothing had happened and asked her to come over. He didn't even mention her outing to the beach with Lauren, let alone ask her how she'd got on.

'Is she that bad?' he asked. 'This Cerise? You make her sound like a monster.'

'She near enough is. And then there's her daughter, Almondine. She's yucky.'

'It'll be a bad do if your dad marries her mother then.'

'*Marries* her?' Johnny was getting ahead of himself, surely. Although Sylvie had done just that as well.

'Well, the way you've been going on –'

'She seems to have got her claws into him,' admitted Holly gloomily.

'Sounds more like fangs.' Johnny seemed to be enjoying the idea.

'It's not just that. She'd eat my dad up.'

'There'd be one thing for it, then, if he did marry her.'

'What's that?'

'Run away from home!'

Holly laughed at her friend as he ran as fast as he could on the spot. It was a tempting thought, and it would solve quite a few of her problems, but it wasn't very practical. Anyway, the Social Services would be after Holly like a shot if she tried to do a runner.

Their discussion was disturbed by the arrival of Johnny's friend Tim, bearing a tennis racket.

'I thought we were on for tennis this morning?' he said to Johnny.

'We are. But I'm giving Holly some coaching first. You can come and watch,' Johnny told him.

Holly would have preferred not to have anyone watching – even Tim, whom she liked. She might make a fool of herself as she'd never been any good at hitting balls in the past. But then she'd thought the same about chess until Johnny had bullied her into it. Nina was always telling her to stand up to Johnny more.

'Give him as good as you get!'

She was getting better at it.

They were ready to leave for the tennis courts when Lauren arrived at the front door to ask if Holly was there and would she like to do something with her.

'Come and join us,' said Johnny. 'Got a tennis racket?'

Lauren leapt at the idea, and ran to fetch it. Holly's spirits tumbled. She just knew that Lauren would turn out to be a brilliant tennis player, and she was right. She seemed to be able to play easily with long, smooth strokes, as if her racket was an extension of her long arm.

Holly's frantic swipes at the ball couldn't have been more different. It usually sailed past her without her even seeing it. Admittedly she hadn't played often before. Only once or twice.

While Lauren played Tim, Holly had a coaching session with Johnny and managed to miss most of the balls that he lobbed at her. Those she did connect with went straight into the bottom of the net.

'Take your time,' he yelled. 'Wait! Don't rush at it. Let it come to you more.'

'I'm no use at this.' Holly couldn't help noticing Lauren leaping around the next court like a gazelle. Tim didn't know what had hit him.

'You're not holding your racket the way I told you.' Johnny came round the net to show her. They played for another few minutes until Holly pleaded exhaustion.

All Holly wanted to do was go home and read a book. Instead she had to sit at the side of the court with Tim while Lauren beat Johnny, who didn't like that at all.

'She's a natural,' said Tim admiringly as Lauren gave a little victory dance.

Holly didn't feel she was a natural at anything, except reading, perhaps.

When they went back to Johnny's house Nina gave them a big picnic in the back garden. She was very good at picnics.

They squatted on a rug on the grass, with Lauren re-enacting her best shots. Holly fell quiet and didn't contribute much to the chatter. She didn't feel she had much to say. She'd never really been part of a group of friends before. In Glasgow she'd only had one school friend, Ellie, but they hadn't seen each other much out of school. Lauren and the two boys seemed to have so much to say and they talked and laughed loudly and butted in on each other. There never seemed to be enough space for Holly. After a while she got up and slid away quietly, back into the house. They wouldn't notice she'd gone.

Nina was in the kitchen making an apple tart. She said she enjoyed baking after a long spell of writing. It relaxed her.

'Hello, love,' she said as Holly came in. 'How are you getting on out there? Bit overpowering, are they?'

Holly shrugged. 'A bit.'

'You're OK, you don't have to be talking at the top of your voice. I'm always telling Johnny he doesn't have to shout, I'm not deaf. Could you measure out some of that plain flour for me?'

The back door opened and Johnny came in to get a glass of water.

'There you are,' he said to Holly. 'I wondered where you'd got to. Are you coming out then? I'm going to set up the ping-pong table in the garden.'

Ping-pinny! More bats and balls. Holly sighed.

'Come on!' he urged. 'We need you to make up a foursome.'

'I'll come in a minute.'

'Don't be long!'

'And don't you be so bossy,' said his mother.

Holly was toying with the idea of talking to Nina about the package now hidden in her bottom drawer.

She was dying to talk to somebody, apart from Sylvie. Sometimes she thought her head was going to burst.

But Sylvie didn't want Holly to say a word to Nina, sure that Nina would only go and tell Holly's dad. She was probably right. And if Nina did tell her dad he might go to the police. But would he, if he knew it could get her mum into trouble? *Big* trouble.

'He might because he'd be so angry,' said Sylvie. 'And he will be angry, you know that. He'll hit the roof when he finds out.'

Holly couldn't decide.

'Best to say nothing,' advised Sylvie. 'We've got to solve this ourselves. It's our secret.'

This was the kind of secret Holly would rather not have. It was burning her up.

Her mobile rang, startling her. She'd been miles away. She looked to see who the caller was.

'It's my mum,' she said.

'Better answer it then,' said Nina and Holly couldn't exactly say she didn't want to.

'Holly, are you there?'

Holly didn't like the sound of Mum's voice. It was high pitched and urgent.

'I'm at Nina's.'

'Can you go somewhere –' Sharon dropped her voice, '– sort of private? Where nobody can hear you? Maybe out in the garden? You said they had a big garden, didn't you?'

Holly thought of the garden with Johnny, Tim and Lauren out there making a racket.

'Hang on a minute, Mum.'

'Why don't you take your call in the dining room,' suggested Nina in a whisper, pointing down the hallway. 'You'll get some peace in there.'

Holly took her advice. It was quiet and still in the room, with everything in order. It was the tidiest room in the house. The Nightingale family usually ate in the kitchen, unless they had guests, posh guests.

She closed the door behind her. Now she could talk.

'What's wrong, Mum?' she asked. As if she didn't know!

'You mind the package Lenny gave me?'

Holly gulped. How could she forget it? Her faint hopes that anyone else had were shattered.

'Do you, Holly?'

'Yes, Mum.'

'It must have fallen out my bag in the station. It was there when I was doing my make-up, I remember seeing it . . .'

Holly swallowed.

'Holly, you didn't happen to pick it up by any chance, did you? While I was talking to your dad.'

'No.' Holly could hardly breathe. What a liar she was!

'Are you sure?

Holly didn't answer.

'You see,' Sharon carried on, 'I went back down to the station with Jacko to have a look around and that guy – the one who was clearing the tables, the flirty one – told me he'd seen a package under the table.'

'Oh . . . he never mentioned.'

'And he said –' Sharon paused for breath, '– he said he was sure he saw you pick it up.'

Holly closed her eyes. There was no point in trying to pretend.

'What did you do with it, Holly? Tell me! You've got to tell me!'

'I put it in my bag,' Holly said in a very small voice. 'It was an accident! I wasn't looking what I was doing . . . I meant to put it in yours.'

There was a pause at the other end of the line before Sharon rallied.

'OK. So what have you done with it?'

'Think!' said Sylvie.

'I threw it in the bin.' Holly just wanted this mess to go away.

'The bin! Whereabouts?'

'In the street.'

'Hell's bells, Holly!' cried Sharon. 'Lenny'll kill me when he finds out. It's worth a lot of money. Jacko's after him for that package. He's had to go and lie low with a friend.' Her voice broke. 'Jacko and his men came into our flat and trashed it. They turned over everything lookin' for the stuff.'

Holly was feeling sick now. 'But what about you, Mum? Are you all right? Did they hurt you?'

'I wasn't there, thank goodness. I'm staying with my pal Chrissie who works at the *Spike* with me.'

'Don't go back to the flat, Mum!'

'Don't worry, I won't go near the place. But why did you do that? Put it in the bin?' Sharon groaned. 'Why didn't you just hang onto it, love? You must have known it was important.'

'I wanted rid of it, Mum.'

'So you knew there was something bad in there?' Sharon sounded as if she was talking to a toddler.

'I'm not daft, Mum! I knew it wasn't sweeties, didn't I? I wanted you out of it. I didn't want you to get into trouble,' said Holly.

'I'm in plenty now! It was worth a bomb, that lot. It wasn't cheap. Jacko won't let it go. He is never goin' tae believe me when I tell him it's been dumped. He thinks Lenny is double-crossing him.' Sharon gave out a long sigh. 'Oh, I'm real sorry, pet, I shouldne be goin' on at you. I feel terrible. You shouldne be mixed up with any of this. I never wanted to be. Lenny's a fool.'

'We'll agree with that,' said Sylvie.

'But he's not really bad,' insisted Sharon. 'I mean he's not in the same league as Jacko. That man is bad news through and through.' She sounded tearful.

'He wouldn't come after you, would he?' asked Holly. She could feel her heart thumping.

'Dinne you bother your head about it. I'll sort it out somehow,' said Sharon, although she didn't sound confident. 'I'll tell Jacko somebody lifted it in the station.' She let out another sigh. 'I'd better go. My battery's running low. I'm needin' to charge it. Look, I'll see you Sunday, pet. Like we planned. Look forward to it.' She rang off. It was always the same with Mum.

Holly stood in the Nightingales' posh dining room and stared at her phone. What a mess. And what *was* she going to do with the stuff? She was in possession of it now, wasn't she? She couldn't pretend that the package was a gift from Lenny to Jacko for his birthday, could she? She knew it must be drugs. Did that not make her a criminal now?

She'd read in the *Edinburgh Evening News* about people caught 'in possession of illegal substances', or 'handling stolen goods'. They'd been sent to prison. She could never have imagined that one day she might be one of them.

Fifteen

The package hidden in her bottom drawer was all that Holly could think about the next day. She'd thought about asking Nina what she should do, but there was never a moment without either Johnny or Lauren or Tim being around. She didn't want Nina to think Mum was in yet more trouble, not after all the bother earlier that year when Nina had had to take care of Holly until Dad came home. Holly wouldn't leave the flat, making an excuse when Johnny rang to invite her over. She even found herself pretending she had a cold when Nina phoned to check she was all right.

'If you were careful,' said Sylvie, 'flushing the stuff down the loo might be easiest to do. It would leave no trace.'

Unless Holly messed it up of course. She'd have to cut the packet open first and that could be tricky. It was so well wrapped. She might get the stuff all over the place.

'You could wear rubber gloves.' Sylvie always had an answer. 'Your dad's got a pair in the hall cupboard that he uses for dirty work.'

But Holly was worried they'd be too big for her, make her clumsy.

'You could buy a smaller pair in the chemist.'

'They still might slip on the packet. I'd have to manage a pair of scissors too.' Holly could imagine herself with white powder all over her jeans and the bathroom floor. She was as sure as she could be that the package contained drugs – she imagined it would be all powdery and white.

'What if it's not drugs?' asked Sylvie.

'What else could it be?'

'Sugar?'

'They wouldn't be in such a tizz over a packet of sugar, would they? That's not illegal. There's no way Jacko would be worried about getting a bag of sugar back.'

'Well whatever it is, it would be easy enough to dump it in the bin at the other end of the street,' suggested Sylvie.

'But what about my fingerprints?' The police were forever searching through rubbish bins on the telly.

'They wouldn't suspect you. Why should they? And you live miles away – well, quite a way – from the scene of the crime.'

'My mum's prints –' Holly stopped. Would the police have a record of Sharon's fingerprints? Lenny had been charged with possession of drugs she remembered, but her mum had never said anything about being an accomplice.

'They would only keep her fingerprints if she had been involved in a crime,' said Sylvie. 'Then they'd have them in their files.'

'My mum's honest! She wouldn't commit a crime.' But as soon as the thought came into Holly's head she knew that she couldn't be sure of that. She had to admit that it was possible. Her head was revolving like a merry-go-round. No, more like a waltzer, spinning in and out and around. She'd only ever ridden on one once. With

Sharon, of course. Once had been enough. The ride had frightened the wits out of her, but Sharon loved it so much that she had immediately joined the queue to take the ride all over again.

'There is something else you could do of course,' mused Sylvie.

'What's that?'

'Give the package back to your mum.'

Holly had already thought of that, but she had put it to the back of her mind. She couldn't help imagining her mum sitting on a Glasgow train with the bag on her knee and arriving in Queen Street Station just as two policemen went past. They might have a sniffer dog with them.

'It's not very likely,' said Sylvie.

'How do you know? Just because you've never seen a sniffer dog in the station. Doesn't mean there aren't any.'

'OK! I was just guessing. But one thing, though, if you did give the bag back to your mum –'

'What?'

'She could hand it over, like she was supposed to that day you were in Glasgow. It would get her off the hook with Lenny and Jacko. She'd be in the clear with them.'

Holly immediately felt a sense of relief. Sylvie was right. Mum would be safe then. Why hadn't she thought of that before? The quickest way out of this mess was not to pretend she couldn't do anything, but to make something happen so quickly that it would soon be over.

'So the most important thing,' said Sylvie, 'is to get your mum out of trouble. Right?'

'Right.'

'We know it'd be a bad thing to let the stuff go, for then it could be sold on. Kids might buy it. And then it'd be our fault. Or partly.'

Holly felt slightly sick at the thought.

'We can't help who might buy it though, can we?' she said uneasily. She had seen films about drug dealing at school. It was a horrible, frightening business. The policeman who had come to Holly's school told her class that dealers picked on the weakest people. Afterwards, one of the girls bragged in the playground about smoking something or other, but you couldn't believe half of what she said. She was always telling fibs. Dad said the girl probably wanted attention. Holly thought boasting about taking drugs was an odd way to get it.

Holly's thoughts went round and round in her head.

But she was a bit clearer now. Her main concern was to prevent her mum from being sucked into a horrible situation. Holly didn't think Lenny would harm Mum, but Jacko might. What if he were to beat her up? She shuddered at the thought of Jacko whacking her mum and bruising her lovely face.

Holly closed her eyes. Her head was thumping and she felt as if she was perched on the edge of an aeroplane, just about to do her first parachute jump. Her life had sometimes been quite complicated in the past, but nothing compared to the situation in which she found herself now.

'I'm going to give it back to Mum on Sunday.'

The decision was made.

There were no more difficult decisions to be taken after that, which was a relief. Holly went to the Nightingales' the next day and Johnny didn't mention tennis or coaching again. Holly found she was better at table tennis. It seemed easier somehow to make contact with the ball and you didn't have to run about all over the place. Lauren and Tim turned up that afternoon as usual. Holly had to admit that they were getting on quite well, the four of them.

That evening, Holly and her dad went downstairs to Anna's for supper. They had a nice time. Anna had made lasagne with a crispy salad to go with it and apple sponge for pudding and Holly's dad had taken a bottle of wine. He and Anna drank a few glasses and became quite merry.

'She'd be better for him than Cerise,' said Sylvie, when they were back upstairs. 'She's a better cook too.'

'He doesn't need anybody,' said Holly firmly.

There was no mention of Cerise from Dad, though Holly thought he might have spoken to her again on the phone. He'd gone into his bedroom and closed the door decisively and then she'd heard the low murmur of his voice. The day before too, he had been a little late back from work but she didn't ask where he'd been. She didn't want to know.

On Saturday, Holly spent the whole day with her dad. 'This is our day, love.'

He took her out for lunch down to the port at Leith.

They had a table outside, looking over the water, just along from where she'd had the hot chocolate with Anna. After they'd finished eating they sat on for a while watching the people coming and going.

'I'm going birdwatching with Anna tomorrow,' Dad said. 'At the John Muir Trust.'

Holly nodded. The news didn't come as a surprise. She wasn't sure how she felt about it, but she wasn't exactly upset.

'You'll be with your mum.'

Of course, tomorrow was Sunday! Holly had almost put it out of her head. Though she was looking forward to seeing her mum, of course. Finally she'd be able to get rid of the package.

'What are you thinking of, love?' asked Dad.

'Nothing.'

'You looked far away. Anything bothering you?'

'No, I'd just kind of forgotten tomorrow was Sunday.'

Her dad gave her an odd look, then put his hand over hers. 'You'd tell me if there was anything the matter, wouldn't you?'

She nodded.

'It's difficult for you being without your mum, I'm aware of that, but you know you couldn't possibly live with her.'

She really didn't want to talk about it. 'It's all right, Dad. Honest it is. I like living with you.'

He squeezed her hand and stood up. 'Shall we go?'

Sunday dawned fine and clear. Holly's dad was up early. He hummed while he packed his binoculars and dusted down his camping stool. Anna was bringing a picnic, he said, and he was taking a flask of coffee and some biscuits.

'That sounds good,' said Holly. She almost wished she was going with them. There was a knot at the bottom of her stomach.

'I expect your mum will take you somewhere nice for lunch. Best get yourself ready then. We've to meet her at twelve. That's if she's there on time of course,' her dad added, but he was smiling.

Holly went into her room and closed the door.

'You've got to do it!' ordered Sylvie. 'You have to get Lenny and Jacko off your mum's back.'

Sylvie was right.

Holly squatted down on her hunkers in front of the chest of drawers and pulled out the bottom one. Or tried to. She tugged and tugged but the drawer came out only a tiny bit. It was squint now. One corner stuck out at an angle. She tried to jiggle it back and forth, but it was stuck fast.

'Calm down,' said Sylvie. 'Try again.'

'Holly,' called Dad. 'Are you ready?'

'In a minute.' Holly tried again. She was sweating now. She took hold of the two handles of the drawer and tugged as hard as she possibly could, falling backwards onto the floor with the effort. She scrambled up and had another go. But the drawer just would not budge any further.

And stuck inside it was Lenny's package.

Sixteen

'Holly,' called her dad again. He was getting impatient.

'Coming.'

She tried to shut the drawer this time, but it would not move either in or out. She would just have to leave it. It was a disaster, but she couldn't keep Dad waiting any longer. Holly picked up her bag and went through to the kitchen where her dad was waiting.

'You look a bit red in the face,' he observed. He frowned, came closer to her. 'You're not running a temperature, are you?'

'No, I'm fine.'

He put his hand on her forehead, anyway, just to make sure. He could be a bit of a fusspot. 'You seem all right.'

'I am.'

'Let's go then!'

They took a bus up to the station. Sharon was due in at twelve. And she was! Right on time.

'Must be an all-time first,' said Dad when he saw her coming through the barrier.

Although Holly's mum greeted her with a big hug and picked her off her feet to give her a whirl around, she didn't seem as bubbly as she usually was. 'You're getting to be a big girl, Hol,' said Sharon. 'I won't be able to do that much longer. Pick you up, I mean – you'll never be too big for a hug.'

'I'll leave the two of you then,' said Dad. 'Meet you back here at five.'

Sharon linked her arm through Holly's. 'What would you like to do today, love?'

'Don't mind.'

'I can't buy you much, I'm afraid. I'm a bit short –'

'You don't have to buy me anything,' Holly said quickly.

'It's just with me and Lenny being split up –'

'That's all right, Mum.'

'We could buy ourselves a couple of filled rolls and some juice and take it into the gardens.'

She didn't say anything about the package. But Holly was certain she would want to discuss it. She wasn't looking forward to that conversation.

There were lots of people out enjoying the sunshine in Princes Street Gardens. Many were tourists. They heard voices from different countries as they walked. Germany. France. Holly caught that one. They'd been learning French at school. Then there was a man speaking Italian. Or maybe Spanish. She wasn't sure. She'd like to learn Spanish so that she could go to Spain, though Sharon said she didn't need to because nearly everyone spoke English there. Holly still thought it would be nice to be able to speak a bit of Spanish. Johnny was studying it at school. Two American tourists walked by, loudly wondering exactly how old Edinburgh Castle was.

'Lenny says he'll take me to Florida,' said Sharon. 'We'll go to Orlando and Disney.'

Holly couldn't believe her ears. Hadn't they split up? But there was no point in trying to get her mum to talk sense when it came to Lenny. Dad had once said Sharon lived in cloud cuckoo land. 'She'll believe anything. That's her problem.'

Still no word from Sharon about the package.

They found a quiet spot and sat down. The castle stood high above them and they could hear the sound of bagpipes and drums. There must be a band playing somewhere in the gardens. Sharon kicked off her shoes, waggled her toes and lay back on the grass. 'It's nice and peaceful here.' She normally didn't care much for peaceful places.

Sharon was definitely quieter than usual and she ate only half her roll, which was unlike her too. She gave the rest to Holly.

'Is everything all right, Mum?' asked Holly finally. She meant, of course, the trouble with Lenny and Jacko but didn't want to spell it out. Her mum understood well enough. She sat up. 'Not really, pet. Jacko's been round to the *Spike* twice asking about you-know-what.'

'What did you say to him?'

'I told him somebody had nicked the stuff from my bag in the station.'

'Did he believe you?'

Sharon shrugged. 'I stuck to my story.'

Holly fiddled with some daisies. All she could think of was that the package that was causing so much trouble was sitting right now in her bottom drawer at the flat. She brooded on that.

'Penny for them?' said Sharon after a while.

Holly's head jerked up.

'What were you thinking about, pet?'

'Oh, just that stuff.'

'That stuff?'

'You know, in the package.'

'You shouldne be thinking about that. Pity, though, you put it in the bin. Not that I'm blaming you, pet –'

'Mum, I didn't!' Holly burst out.

'You didn't what?'

'Didn't put it in the bin.'

'You're kiddin' me on!'

'I'm not!'

'What did you do with it then?'

'Put it in my drawer.'

'*What*? Are you telling me it's actually in your drawer at your dad's, now, this very minute?'

Holly nodded. She'd been worried her mum might be cross, but instead she just looked relieved.

'Does your dad know?'

'Course not.'

Sharon sat up straight. 'Has he gone out?'

'He's away birdwatching. Down to Dunbar.'

'In that case he'll be gone a while.' A light had come into Sharon's eyes. She stood up and brushed some dry grass from her skirt. 'Let's go get it then, kiddo!'

'But the drawer's stuck.'

'How d'you mean *stuck*?'

'I think I got a sweater caught in it. I tugged it really hard but it wouldn't budge.'

'There must be a way to open it. I'll sort it.'

Sharon scrabbled around for her shoes and pushed her feet into them. Holly gathered up the remains of their picnic.

'Don't be wasting time, love. We've got to move.'

'I've got to put these in the bin first,' insisted Holly. Her dad made a fuss about leaving litter lying around.

'Well, be quick about it!' Sharon was geared up, ready to go. She was already making her way across the grass towards the path. Holly caught her up and they climbed the steps from the gardens up to Princes Street together.

'Have you any money on you, love?' asked Sharon. 'We could take a taxi if you did. Be a lot faster than the bus.'

Holly could only fish out a few coins from her pocket. Not enough for a taxi.

'We'll just need to take the bus then,' said her mum. 'Look at the queue!' She ran across the road.

The buses didn't run at full strength on Sundays and the town was busy with shoppers that day. A number in the line were swinging bulging carrier bags.

Sharon tapped her toe restlessly on the pavement and leant out every few seconds to peer along the street to see if a bus was coming.

'That won't make it come any faster,' muttered Holly.

'Dinne have to wait this long for a bus in Glasgae,' said Sharon.

'Away on back there then!' said a man behind them.

Sharon turned and gave him a dirty look.

Holly looked at the ground, her face burning.

They had to wait twenty minutes for a bus and then four came at once.

It was standing room only downstairs and there was no way Sharon would be able to make it up to the top deck in those shoes. She pressed her way towards the back, apologizing loudly, being tutted at by the other passengers as she jostled them. Holly stayed near the front of the bus, tucking herself in as best she could. The bus seemed to stop at every red light and there was a bottleneck of traffic at the east end of Princes Street. Holly could see Mum growing more and more impatient. She made her way back down through the passengers to join Holly.

'Everything's agin us,' she moaned. 'We could have walked it faster.'

Holly could have done but she wasn't sure about her mum. Not with those heels.

Finally, they reached the stop nearest Dad's flat. They half-walked, half-ran up the stairs. Mrs McGinty was at the top, as only to be expected, looking down on them from over the banister, waiting to see who was coming up. Did she just stand there all day every day, wondered Holly, waiting for something to pass judgement on?

'Back again?' she said to Sharon, and then to Holly, 'Your dad not here?'

'Why don't you mind your own business,' snapped Sharon. 'You'll fall over the banister one of these days and end up in the basement.'

The vision of it made Holly giggle, even though she knew it was a bit mean.

Holly unlocked the door of the flat and they went in. Sharon made straight for Holly's room. She took a look at the drawer, kicked off her shoes and kneeled down.

'OK, love, let's have a go at it together. You take one handle and I'll take the other.'

They squatted side by side.

'Ready?' said Sharon, taking hold. 'Pull!'

They pulled and Holly fell backwards as she had done before, but this time she was left with the handle in her hand. The drawer sat there, not having budged a centimetre. It looked as if it was smirking at them. Holly couldn't bear to look at her mum.

'Hell's bells!' cried Sharon in frustration. She thumped the top of the chest with her fist. Holly had never seen her like this.

'If your dad had bought proper furniture, not this cheap ancient stuff . . .' she muttered, rubbing her forehead.

'Listen!' said Holly.

She thought for a moment she'd heard the sound of the front door opening . . . then a cough. She *had*!

'Holy gromoly!' groaned Sharon. 'I thought you said he'd gone birdwatching?'

The door opened behind them. Dad stood there looking down on the pair of them, sprawled on the floor. He stared at the handle in Holly's hand.

'What in the name's going on here?' he asked.

Seventeen

They scrambled to their feet.

'Oh, hello there, Joe,' said Sharon, fumbling for her shoes and pushing her feet back into them. 'Holly brought me down to show me her new clothes.'

'New clothes?' Dad looked unconvinced. He hadn't bought Holly any new clothes recently.

'What are you doing home, Dad?' gabbled Holly. 'I thought you were away for the afternoon?'

'Anna wasn't feeling very well so we packed it in. What's that you've got in your hand, Holly?' He nodded at the drawer handle.

Holly glanced down. 'It just came off.'

'I'll need to sort it.' His voice was very calm. As if he was holding back.

'I'd love a cuppa tea, Joe,' put in Sharon. 'I'm fair parched.'

He raised his eyebrows at her, then led the way into the kitchen. Sharon chirped on about being awful thirsty and that it must be because of the warm day and she hadn't been able to take Holly to a cafe because she was a bit on the short side this week.

'Bills to pay. You know how it is.'

Dad made no response. Holly put the kettle on.

'Want a cup, Dad?'

'Might as well.'

Holly set three mugs out and pulled a carton of milk from the fridge. They sat at the table.

For the briefest of moments, Holly considered blurting out the whole story. Then her mum and dad would have to decide what to do with the package, leaving her out of it. But her dad's expression was so odd that she decided not to risk it. She couldn't bear another row. No, Holly had brought this mess into her dad's flat and she needed to get it out again without him knowing. It was unlikely that he would let her mum go off with a packet of drugs, after all. A part of Holly knew she didn't really want that either, but she didn't see how else to put a stop to the situation.

Sharon was trying to keep a conversation going without much success. Holly felt as if her tongue was tied in knots and her dad was obviously not in a talkative mood. He knew there was something going on.

Eventually Sharon dried up and sipped her tea. Holly wasn't sure what she preferred – the chattering or the uncomfortable silence.

The phone rang, sounding louder than usual. Dad went into the hall to answer it and then Holly heard him take the handset into his bedroom, closing the door behind him.

Holly hoped it wasn't Cerise again but, for the moment, Cerise was the least of her worries.

'Holly,' said Sharon urgently, tapping Holly's arm, 'ask your dad to open the drawer for you. He won't know what's in there. Say you've got a cardie to show me.'

Holly shook her head. 'He's suspicious, Mum.'

'Why should he be?'

Sometimes Holly wondered whether her mum had any common sense. Couldn't she read Dad at all? 'He might see the packet. And then he's bound to ask.'

'We've got to try it. I'm desperate.' Sharon tapped her fingers on the table. 'I can't believe you were daft enough to take it . . .'

Holly glared at her mother. Dad was still on the phone.

'Who's Joe talking to all this time?' asked Sharon.

Holly didn't see any reason not to tell her mother. 'A woman. She's called Cerise.'

'Jings! She must talk plenty.'

'She does. She keeps phoning him.'

'A phone stalker! Why doesn't he tell her to get lost?'

'I don't know. Maybe he likes her.'

Sharon suddenly looked so sad that Holly went on to tell her about the disastrous visit to Cerise's house and they had a good laugh together. They were still laughing when the door opened and Dad came back in.

'What's so funny?' he asked as he sat down. His voice was cool and his face was a little flushed.

Sharon wiped her eyes and smudged her mascara. 'Nothing. Just a wee joke between us.'

Dad looked a bit peeved.

Sharon gave Holly a meaningful look and nudged her foot under the table.

Holly took a deep breath. 'Dad,' she said, 'I can't get my bottom drawer open. It's stuck. Do you think you could fix it for me?'

'Now?'

'I just want to show something to Mum.'

At least that was true.

'Well, OK.' Dad got up a little reluctantly. Holly led the way into her bedroom, leaving Sharon sitting in the kitchen trying not to look as if it had anything to do with her.

'You did make a pig's ear of it,' said Dad when he saw the drawer. 'I'll see what I can do. It's going to be hard to get it open with only one handle.'

He squatted down, took hold of the remaining handle and putting his other hand on the corner of the drawer that was sticking out, he pulled and shoved until he grew brick red in the face. The drawer would not budge.

He sat back on his hunkers pondering what to do. 'I'll need to take a chisel to it. See if I can whittle a bit of that edge away.'

'I'm sorry, Dad.' Holly felt dreadful. Her palms were sweaty.

'What have you got in there?'

'Just sweaters. Fleeces. Winter stuff.'

'You've rammed too much in.'

'I know. Will I get you the chisel from your cupboard?'

'I'm not going to do it now. I'll get round to it later.'

'But I wanted to show Mum – '

'What?'

'Just a sweater,' said Holly tried to sound offhand. She avoided her dad's eye.

'Show her next time.'

He got up and rubbed his knees. Holly knew when she

couldn't argue with him. And if she made much more of it he might become even more suspicious.

They went back to the kitchen. Sharon turned round. 'Any luck?'

Holly shook her head.

'She's made a good job of jamming it,' said Dad.

'That's too bad.' Sharon bit her lip.

'Dad's going to do it later,' put in Holly quickly.

'I guess I'd better be going then.' Sharon stood up and picked up her bag. 'Chum me down the stairs, Holly?'

'Bye then, Sharon,' said Dad, rinsing out the mugs. 'See you next Sunday in the station. Same time?'

Holly closed the door of the flat quietly so as not to alert Mrs McGinty. Neither she nor Sharon spoke at all until they were half way down the stairs.

'When your dad gets the drawer open, you ring me. Straightaway. I need that package.' Holly wanted to point out that since her mum had told everyone Holly had thrown it away there really wasn't a rush, but Sharon was near tears.

'OK. But how will I get it to you?'

'I'll come through.'

'I could meet you off the train.' Holly regretted the offer immediately. That would mean she'd have to carry the package to the station in the bus.

'I'm certainly not coming here,' Sharon said, pointing up towards where Mrs McGinty was usually to be found, waiting. 'I could walk down part way to meet you,' she suggested.

They'd reached the passage to the front door. Sharon

pushed it open and they went out, blinking in the sun.

'We could meet on the corner of Gayfield Square,' suggested Sharon. 'That's about halfway, isn't.'

'But that's where the police hang out, Mum. They've got a station there.'

Sharon half laughed. 'So they have. Further up then?'

They agreed on the corner at the top of the road, across the street from the big cinema complex. Holly could tell her mum was anxious, the way she repeated the instructions three or four times.

They heard footsteps and then the door opened behind them. Out came Anna and Cindy.

'Hi, Holly!'

'Are you feeling better?' asked Holly.

'Yes, thanks. I had a migraine earlier, but it's calmed down so I thought I'd come out for a breath of fresh air.'

'I've heard migraines are awfy things,' said Sharon, quickly. 'Never had one myself.'

'You're lucky!'

'Mum,' said Holly awkwardly, 'this is Anna, our neighbour downstairs.'

'Oh yes, I've heard about you from Holly. You and your dog. Pleased to meet you.'

The two women nodded at each other and Anna said she was pleased to meet Sharon too.

Holly shuffled her feet around. 'You'll need to go, Mum, or you'll miss your train.'

'Oh, there's no rush, love. There's plenty trains to Glasgow, even on Sunday. Every half hour, I think. Or is it fifteen minutes?'

The two women politely discussed the train service to Glasgow and then Anna said she must go as Cindy was tugging at her lead, wanting to be on the move. They went off down the street.

'You'd better get back up to your dad,' said Sharon. 'He'll be wondering where you are. He's probably looking out of the window right now.'

They arched their backs and looked up and there he was. They could just make out the blur of his face.

Sharon sighed. 'See? He doesnae trust me.'

'You can't blame him, can you?' said Holly, quietly.

'No, I suppose not,' Sharon said sadly before she kissed Holly and darted across the road, dodging the traffic to reach the bus stop on the other side. A bus was pulling in. She turned to give Holly a quick wave and a minute later was on board the bus and heading up the hill.

Holly walked back upstairs.

'I got your drawer open,' said her dad.

Eighteen

Holly tried not to fret as they went into her room. The corner of the drawer no longer stuck out.

'I had to chisel a bit off at the edge,' Dad explained. 'You'll need to be careful how you open it. Look!'

Holly held her breath as he squatted down and eased the drawer out.

'I'll put the other handle on later.'

'Thanks, Dad.' Holly wished he would get up now and leave the drawer alone. It was standing open.

'You've got far too much in there. You should take something out. What about that one at the top? You don't need it just now. You've probably grown out of it.'

'I'll have a look later.' Holly was feeling desperate. What if he started to pull all her sweaters out?

'I'll give you a plastic bag and we could take some of your old things to the charity shop.'

'It's OK, Dad.'

But he was already lifting out another one, a thick red winter fleece. 'You definitely won't need to wear this over the summer. Here, take it from me and I'll find a place to store it. This one's plenty big enough yet.'

Holly took it, willing him not to rummage any further.

But he was still studying the drawer and its contents. 'You could put another couple away as well.'

'Want to keep them there. Sometimes it gets cold at night.'

He looked up at her, smiling. 'Not *that* cold.'

'I'd just like to leave them as they are, Dad.' She knew she was beginning to sound quite childish, she'd give herself away if he went on.

'All right, suit yourself.' Dad got up. 'I'll do the handle later. It should screw on again quite easily.'

When he left, Holly collapsed on top of the bed. She felt as if she had run three marathons.

'Don't just lie there!' said Sylvie. 'You'll need to move Lenny's package before your dad comes back to sort the handle.'

Holly vaulted off the bed and looked around the room. Where could she hide the stuff now? Under the bed?

'No!' cried Sylvie. 'Last time he vacuumed he pushed the bed over.

'What about behind the wardrobe?' she suggested. 'He wouldn't move that. It'd be too heavy.'

That seemed as good an idea as any other. There was just enough space behind there for the slim package. Holly yanked out several sweaters, flinging them behind her, until she found what she was looking for. Swiftly she transferred it to its new home. The space between the wall and the back of the wardrobe became narrower towards the floor. The package slotted in neatly about halfway down.

She had just finished when her dad put his head round the door, giving her a fright. She stood in front of the wardrobe as if to protect it.

'What do you fancy for your tea?' he asked. He stopped when he saw the sweaters and fleeces lying higgledy-piggledy all over the floor.

'What are you doing with that lot? I thought you didn't want to be bothered today.'

Holly shrugged. 'I'm sorting them.'

'If you want any more plastic bags let me know. So, what would you like to eat, love? Did you have a proper lunch with your mum?'

'Not really. Just a roll. She'd no money.'

He shook his head, then said, 'What about a Spanish omelette?'

'That'd be great, Dad.'

Holly started to fold up the sweaters.

'I'll leave you to it.' He went out and closed the door.

☆ ★ ☆

After they'd eaten and Holly was doing the washing up, her phone rang – it was Johnny.

'I'll take it in my room. I'll finish the dishes later, Dad.'

Nina Nightingale was planning a trip down to the Borders the next day, to Dryburgh Abbey. She was doing some research for a new book.

'She wonders if you'd like to come too?' asked Johnny.

'I would.' Holly couldn't think of anything better. Anything to get away from here.

'We're leaving early. Nine o'clock. That OK?'

'I'll be ready.'

'Pick you up then.'

Johnny rang off and Holly went through to tell Dad. He was very pleased, telling her it was lovely down there at Dryburgh. He'd gone once to a scout camp when he was her age. He'd had a great time. Holly relaxed for the first time that day as she listened to him reminiscing happily. He didn't often do that, and she enjoyed listening to his stories. He sounded nostalgic.

Their chat was interrupted when Holly's mobile buzzed with a text. It was from her mum.

Any luck? Holly turned the phone face down on the table. She really didn't want to do this now. Or ever.

The house phone rang and Holly answered, knowing exactly who it would be.

'Hang on a minute, Mum. I'll go into my room.'

Dad raised his eyebrows, but he smiled at her, and picked up his newspaper.

Holly made sure she closed the door properly.

'Did your dad get it open?' asked Sharon, the moment Holly was settled.

'Yes, he did.'

'Thank goodness for that! What've you done with the stuff? Did you take it out the drawer?'

'Put it behind the wardrobe.'

'Is that safe?'

'Safe as anywhere.'

'Look then, love, I'll come through in the morn. I could meet you at eleven o'clock on the corner. Your dad'll be away at his work.'

'I can't, Mum. I've just said I'll go out with Nina and Johnny tomorrow.'

'Phone them back and tell them you can't.'

Holly thought she might just burst into tears. 'But, Mum, I want to go. They're going to visit Dryburgh Abbey.'

'Where in the name's that?'

'Down the Borders.'

'You can go and see a dusty old abbey any time. If you want to,' added Sharon doubtfully. She hadn't much interest in history, Holly remembered.

'I can't. Nina's doing research. It's got to be tomorrow. Anyway, Dad would want to know why I changed my mind. He'd suspect something was going on. In fact I'm sure he already suspects.'

Sharon sighed heavily. 'You could tell them that you'd arranged to see another friend and had forgotten.'

'I haven't got any other friends.'

'What about that girl – what's her name? Laura?'

'Lauren – and she lives next door to the Nightingales.'

Sharon was silent for a moment, then said, 'If you're going to the Borders you'll be back late, I expect. Oh well, I suppose it'll have to wait till Tuesday, as long as you think it's safe behind the wardrobe. I don't like the idea of you having it in your room at all. What if your dad went in to look round?'

'He won't.' Holly tried to sound more confident than she felt. But Dad would be out to work tomorrow. He wouldn't be doing any housework.

'Oh, all right. Let's say Tuesday then. Same arrangement?'

'OK.'

'Love you, pet.'

'Love you, Mum.' And she did, very much. She just wished her mum could be a little less trouble sometimes.

☆ ☆ ☆

Monday was another sunny day.

'It's amazing,' said Nina. 'Great spell of weather for a change.'

Holly loved spending so much time out of doors. She'd never played out in the street much in Glasgow, instead, she'd mostly stayed indoors, reading – and waiting for Sharon to come back.

Holly sat in the front seat of the car beside Nina while Johnny lounged in the back playing with his smartphone. Holly didn't have one. Her dad said he couldn't afford it, and anyway, Holly suspected that he didn't approve of them. And her old mobile was perfectly adequate, really.

As they drove, Nina told her a bit about the book she was planning. It wouldn't be set in the 12th century when the abbey had been built, but it would have a mystery connected with it. What was best of all was that Sylvie would feature in it. Holly was aware that Sylvie hadn't been around much recently. There had been so much going on. In a way she was relieved not to have her chirping away, bossing Holly around. But it was good to know that Nina had plans for her.

They went on a quick tour round the abbey, which Johnny only just tolerated. He complained that he'd been dragged round there before, at least twice.

'It's only ruins,' he protested. He had brought a mini chess set with him and kept trying to persuade Holly to play.

'Plenty of time for that,' said his mother.

Holly would have liked to spend longer with Nina for she was good at bringing the place alive, explaining what the rooms were for and how the monks would have lived all those centuries before. But Johnny was restless. He always was. After they'd had a drink and a biscuit out of Nina's wicker hamper he spread a rug on a grassy patch and they sprawled on it with the chess set, leaving Nina to wander in peace. Some tourists came and went but there was something about the place that meant they were quiet and respectful of the history.

After a late lunch they started home. This time Holly sat in the back with Johnny. He fiddled with his phone again and she gazed out of the window. She felt sleepy. But happy. It had been lovely to get away from everything for the day. Nina was quiet too, perhaps thinking of her story.

'You could come back and eat with us with us if you like, Holly,' said Nina as they reached the outskirts of Edinburgh. 'But maybe your dad will be expecting you?'

'He will.' Holly had promised him that she would cook that evening. Sausages, beans and oven chips. She could manage that.

Nina pulled up outside Holly's door. 'Got your key?'

'Yes. Thanks, Nina. I really liked the abbey.'

'See you tomorrow,' said Johnny.

'I can't come over till the afternoon.'

'Why not?'

'Got to do something in the morning.'

'What?'

'Johnny, stop cross-questioning Holly!' said Nina, laughing. 'It's her own business.'

'It's not though, is it?' said Sylvie. 'It's your mum's. And Lenny's. And it's because of him that you've got to carry that bag all the way up the street tomorrow.'

Holly shut Sylvie up. She didn't want to be reminded.

'See you tomorrow, at some point,' said Nina.

Holly waved them off and turned towards her door. There was a police car double parked close by. She didn't pay much attention to it but as soon as she entered the stair she realised that something was wrong.

Nineteen

There were voices floating down from above, male and female, and Cindy was barking. Holly raced up the stairs, passing Anna's door, which stood slightly ajar.

Anna was on the top landing along with Mrs McGinty and two policemen.

'What is it?' cried Holly, running as fast as she could. 'What's happening?'

Mrs McGinty found her voice first. 'Your flat's been broken into.' She sounded almost pleased.

'Thank you, Mrs McGinty,' said Anna, with a slight edge to her voice. 'This is Holly, officer.' She put an arm round Holly's shoulder and turned to the two police constables. 'As I told you, she lives here with her dad, Joe Hamilton.'

'Is my dad all right?' cried Holly.

'He's fine,' said Anna. 'He's still at work, isn't he?' She smiled reassuringly.

'We've got a couple of questions we'd like to ask you, Holly,' said the younger policeman. 'I'm Constable Hunter, and this is my boss, Inspector Morgan.'

Holly nodded at them both. She didn't know whether you were supposed to shake hands with a policeman.

Constable Hunter flipped over a page of his notebook. 'Can you confirm your father's name is Joe Hamilton?'

'Yes.'

Mrs McGinty couldn't hold her tongue any longer. 'It was me that called the police, Holly. I saw the man plain as plain.'

Inspector Morgan interrupted her. 'We need to get in touch with your dad, Holly. Where would he be?'

Holly felt all whirled around and upside down after coming back from the peace of the abbey to all this. She swallowed hard. 'At work. But he should be on his way home by now. Unless he's gone shopping.'

'Can you call him?'

Holly nodded. She took out her mobile and tried his number.

No reply. It went to the answering service, but she didn't leave a message.

'He's not answering. He could be driving.'

'We don't want to go into the flat until he's had a chance to look around and see if anything's been taken,' Inspector Morgan explained.

Holly looked at the door now for the first time. It was splintered and standing wide open.

'Don't worry, Holly,' said Anna, patting her shoulder. 'It seems like he didn't have time to take anything.'

Mrs McGinty butted in again. 'I heard a noise and saw him through the peephole. I was on to the police immediately. I wasted no time.'

'That was the right thing to do,' said the younger policeman. 'Never try to tackle anyone yourself.'

The police would have got here quickly since they had a station not far up the street.

'I opened the door and shouted "Polis!" at him,' continued Mrs McGinty. 'That stopped him in his tracks, I can tell you! He'd only got in a couple of minutes. When he saw me at my door he turned tail and fled. I was able to give the police a good description.'

'You were indeed,' confirmed the inspector, exchanging a glance with his partner. 'You were very helpful, Mrs McGinty.'

She was loving this. 'There's such a lot of coming and going on these stairs these days . . . Wonder what the burglar could have been looking for,' the old lady mused.

Holly was also wondering that. That, and who the burglar might have been. She had a queasy feeling in the pit of her stomach that she knew exactly who it might have been. But surely her mum wouldn't have sent Lenny over to get the package? Or perhaps she hadn't sent him – perhaps he'd taken matters into his own hands.

They heard the bottom door open and then bang shut. Holly looked over the banisters.

'It's my dad,' she said, relieved.

He came steadily up the stairs, carrying a shopping bag in either hand. There was a small bald patch on the top of his head that Holly hadn't noticed before. When he glanced up and saw the group assembled at the top of the stairs peering down at him he paused for a moment, a frown on his face, before beginning to run.

'What's going on?' he shouted.

'It's all right, Mr Hamilton,' said the constable. 'Everything's under control.'

Holly's dad was even more out of breath than usual by the time he reached the top step. He dropped the two bags of shopping at his feet and pulled Holly into a hug.

'Are you all right, love?'

'I'm fine, Dad. I've just got back.'

'You had a break-in,' Mrs McGinty informed him. 'I got the polis. I phoned them. I got a very good look at him, I can tell you!'

Inspector Morgan cut her off. 'Yes, well, maybe we can all go inside now.'

That did not include Mrs McGinty. She looked miffed.

'We've got your statement, mam,' said the constable. 'We'll come in afterwards so that I can read it through to you.'

Mrs McGinty was forced to retreat – though Holly knew that she would leave her door ajar so that she could overhear anything.

'I'll leave you to it,' said Anna, heading back down stairs. 'I didn't see the man myself so I wouldn't be of any help. He'd gone before I came up. Let me know if there's anything I can do.'

Holly's dad was surveying the damaged door and shaking his head. 'Who'd want to come all the way up here to break in?'

'Top flats are often targeted,' said the policeman. 'Burglars feel they can work away up here without anyone coming past.'

Burglars obviously didn't take into account the possibility of having a Mrs McGinty living across the landing.

Once they'd all gone into the flat, Holly's dad closed the door as best he could.

'We'd like you to take a look round now, Mr Hamilton,' said the policeman in charge, 'and you can let us know if anything is missing or has been tampered with. You might go with him, Holly.'

Holly and her dad went from room to room. It didn't take long since they only had four rooms, including the kitchen. Nothing looked as if it had been disturbed. Her dad opened all the drawers in his room and told Holly to do the same in hers. When they were checking her bedroom, Holly longed to take a quick peek behind her wardrobe but dared not. Dad would have asked what she was up to.

They rejoined the policemen in the living room.

'Nothing's been taken as far as we can tell,' Dad reported. 'I don't have a lot to take.'

'I think Mrs McGinty saved your bacon,' said the constable.

'It's good she's a snoop,' said Dad, with a small smile. 'At times.'

'Have you got insurance, Mr Hamilton?' Her dad nodded. 'You'll get your door mended and paid for, then and be none the worse for it,' the inspector said.

Holly wasn't so sure about that. She had a terrible feeling about the whole business.

'So Mrs McGinty was able to give you a good description of him, constable?' said Dad.

'She certainly did.' Constable Hunter took out his notebook. 'Medium height, on the skinny side, sharp features. Possibly mid-twenties. Flowing syrupy-coloured hair down to his shoulders. That's how Mrs McGinty described it. Syrupy-coloured.'

Lenny.

Holly thought she might choke. It couldn't be! Surely, *surely*, her mum wouldn't have told Lenny and asked him to come and break into their flat?

'What's up, pet?' asked her dad.

'Nothing.'

'You went awful pale there.'

'Maybe gave you a bit of a fright, eh, Holly?' said the constable. 'Seeing your house broken into? Don't worry, though. He'll be well away and he won't be back but we'll be looking out our records to see if we can find a match. He won't have targeted your flat deliberately.'

'That's usually the way. You were just unlucky,' added the inspector.

'You can say that again,' said Dad.

The officers looked around for obvious fingerprints, but they didn't sound very hopeful. Eventually, they left and Dad phoned a friend, a joiner, who came round and patched the door up to make it safe for the night.

Holly waited until they'd eaten and Dad had settled down in front of the telly before she went into her room. She was desperate to know, but there was a large part of her that didn't want to find out. She didn't know if she'd be disappointed or pleased – it would be so much easier if Lenny had just taken the package . . . But when she got a chance to look, there it was, tucked behind the wardrobe, exactly where she'd put it. Holly stared at it for a moment, then took out her mobile. Her dad was still watching television so there wasn't much chance he would overhear her. She hoped to be in time to catch her mum before she went to the *Spike*. She was.

'Oh, hi, pet. Can't speak for long. Have to get going in a minute or I'll be late.'

'Need to speak to you.'

'Better be quick. Just doing my face.'

Holly could hear the noise of perfume being sprayed. 'Mum, did you send Lenny over to look for his stuff?'

There was total silence from the other end. Then Sharon squealed, 'What do you mean – did I send Lenny over? Course I didn't. Why are you askin'? Has he been to see you?'

'Somebody broke into our flat this afternoon, Mum.'

Sharon was silent again

Holly went on, 'Mrs McGinty heard him and called the police.'

'Nosey old so-and-so,' muttered Sharon, but Holly wasn't in the mood.

'She saw him, Mum.'

'She did?'

'She got a good look.'

'So? It's not as if she took a photo, is it?' Sharon tried to make a joke of it, but Holly knew from her voice that she was frightened.

'He scarpered. Mum, the man she described did sound awful like Lenny. You didn't say anything to him, did you? You know, about . . . well, you know.'

'I might have mentioned it.'

Holly squeezed her eyes closed. '*Mentioned* it?' she demanded.

'Don't be angry with me, Holly. It was to get him off my back, love. He was phoning me every two minutes at my work. He even came round to see me at the *Spike*. He was harassing me. I just told him that the stuff was safe and sound at the back of your wardrobe and he needn't worry cos you'd be handing it over to me tomorrow.'

'I can't believe you did that,' said Holly. But the worst thing was that she *could*.

'I wouldn't have had to if you hadn't taken the stuff,' Sharon said sharply. 'And anyway, I didn't think he'd try to go and get it himself,' she added.

Holly thought for a moment. 'How did he know where I lived?' she asked.

'He knew roughly. He knew it was Leith Walk. He must have read the doorbells.'

Holly didn't like the tone of Sharon's voice. 'You're not telling me a fib, are you, Mum?'

Sharon cleared her throat. 'Well, he did come to meet me one time after I'd been to see you. Just that once, though.'

'It *must* have been him, then, who broke in.' Holly was furious now.

'I didn't tell him to do it! Honest I didn't, pet.' There was a pause before Sharon asked, 'Did he get it?'

'No. Mrs McGinty was too quick for him. She was already calling the police just as he was breaking down the door.'

'Trust her!'

'Our door's all splintered. We've got to get a new one.' Didn't Mum realise how serious this was?

'I'm sorry about that, pet. I bet your dad wasn't pleased.'

'Not *too* pleased,' said Holly. How did she expect him to feel?

'I'll meet you tomorrow, though, will I, pet, like we arranged? Eleven o'clock, opposite the cinema?'

'I suppose so,' said Holly. There was nothing else she could do.

'With the package. Och, I'm real sorry, love.'

'It's all right.'

'I'd better fly or I'll be late.' The line went dead.

Holly sat on the bed and stared at the mobile in her lap.

Twenty

'What if the police do catch him?' said Sylvie. 'And what if he clypes on her? Spills the beans. And on you?'

Holly felt sure Lenny would clype on Sharon if he was cross-questioned.

'He's a wimp,' said Sylvie. She was right, as usual.

Holly did another check on the bag, to reassure herself that it really was still there behind the wardrobe, before going back to join her dad.

'Don't be worried that the guy will come back, love,' he said. 'Come and watch this film with me. Let's just try and relax.'

But Holly couldn't relax. Her mind was buzzing. Sharon wouldn't be able to resist telling Lenny that Mrs McGinty had given the police such a good description, she was sure of it. So now he'd know the police were after him, Lenny would be able to prepare himself by working out how to blame Sharon. But then again, he hadn't stolen anything and Holly guessed the police had other crimes to follow up. More serious ones. Perhaps they'd put this one at the bottom of the pile. Holly felt slightly comforted by that. She'd love Lenny to be arrested but not for this particular crime.

The film ended. 'I've seen it before, but it still makes me laugh,' Dad said. 'Cup of tea?'

Holly nodded. 'Yes, please.' She tried to make herself cheer up a bit.

But when Dad came back with the tea, he gave her something else to worry about.

'Why don't I take tomorrow off?' he said. 'I want to be here when they fit the new door. Once that's done we could go off and do something together.'

'I said I'd go to Johnny's for lunch,' Holly told him without really thinking. 'Tim and Lauren are coming round too, and we're probably going to play rounders on the Meadows.'

'Good,' said Dad. 'I'm glad you'll be out in the fresh air, and I'm not sure when they're coming with the new door. Maybe we could go out in the evening. To the cinema? See? Every cloud has a silver lining.'

Holly knew that he was being kind, but now he'd be at home when Holly should be setting out to meet her mum. She wished she hadn't told him when she was going over to the Nightingales'. Now Dad would want to know where she was going. He always did.

'What will you tell him?' asked Sylvie.

Holly had no idea.

'Better find one then,' said Sylvie.

Holly slept very badly that night. Her mind just wouldn't let her calm down. They had breakfast together in the morning, Holly and her dad. He cooked bacon and eggs, she made the toast and set the table.

'So you're going to the Nightingales'?' asked Dad.

'Yes, for lunch and the afternoon. I'm not sure about the rounders . . .' Holly made a face and Dad laughed.

'You'll be just fine,' he told her. 'It's a great game. And what about this morning?' he asked.

'I thought I might go to the library.' Holly concentrated on buttering her toast. 'I need to change my books. I've read them all.'

'Good idea,' said her dad. He approved of going to the library. He wasn't a great reader himself, but he liked the fact that Holly was.

In the end, the joiner arrived around half past nine. Holly went into her room and collected up her library books. There were eight of them, mostly hardbacks. It was going to be quite a squeeze to fit them in her bag. Sylvie began one of her interrogations, asking Holly questions she really didn't want to have to think about.

'Will you put them in the same bag as Lenny's package?'

'Haven't decided.'

'You'll have to be careful not to pull it out at the same time as the books.'

'Nobody will know what it is.'

'It might burst open.'

Holly's stomach collapsed at the thought of white powder cascading all over the library counter. She thought for a minute. There was a canvas shopping bag that her dad usually took to the supermarket. Holly went to fetch it. Her dad was busy with the joiner – they were having problems taking the door off – so he didn't even notice what she was doing.

'Best put the packet at the bottom,' advised Sylvie. 'And leave it in its plastic bag.'

Holly planned to go to the library first, turn in her books and pick two or three more, rather than the usual eight. That meant that she wasn't telling Dad a whole new set of lies. As it was, the bag would be heavy to carry all the way up the street. She planned to set out just after ten. That would give her time to go to the library and make it up the street in time to meet Mum.

'Now for that packet,' said Sylvie.

Holly went to the wardrobe and put her hand round the back. Just as her fingers touched the package the door opened, making her jump and withdraw her hand. Her dad looked in.

'I'm going out to get a new handle for the back of the door.' He stopped. 'What are you doing?'

Holly's face burned. 'Nothing.'

Dad looked at the bag on the floor. 'I could give you a lift to the library. You've got quite a load of books there.'

'It's all right, Dad. It's not far.'

'OK then. See you later.'

He left. She heard him bid the joiner goodbye. Holly wiped her forehead with the back of her hand. She felt as if she had a temperature.

'He's gone,' said Sylvie. 'Relax.'

Easy for her to say!

Holly went back to the wardrobe. For a horrible moment she thought the package had disappeared. Then she saw that it was lying further down. She must have knocked it when she put her hand in earlier. It was wedged in at an awkward angle now. Her arm couldn't reach that far.

'I can't get at it,' she cried. 'It's stuck.' Tears of frustration filled Holly's eyes.

'What about your dad's umbrella?' said Sylvie. 'It's got a long handle.'

Holly rushed off and found it propped inside the front door.

'Don't think it's going to rain,' said the joiner cheerfully. He was sanding the door jamb.

'No. But you never know.'

Holly scuttled back to the bedroom before he could ask any questions.

She inserted the handle of the umbrella along the back of the wardrobe and raked about until it made contact with the bag. Then slowly she tugged. Bit by bit it moved towards her until she was able to get her fingers in and snatch it. She wiped her forehead again.

She placed the package at the bottom of the canvas bag and carefully laid the eight library books on top.

'Need to watch your time,' Sylvie reminded her.

Holly was ready to scream. As if she needed Sylvie to remind her!

'Off out?' asked the joiner.

'Going to the library.'

'Read a lot?'

'Yes.' She edged passed him and made her way down the stairs to the bottom door. There was no sign of Mrs McGinty. What a relief! She must be out shopping. The bag was heavy, and now that she was outside she realised that it was quite a warm day. Holly felt her shoulders being pulled downwards. She was glad when she finally reached the library and checked the books in.

'Read them all?' asked the librarian.

'Yes.'

'Jolly good. We've got some new books in this week. Just shelved them this morning.'

Holly moved on into the body of the library, making for the children's section. A woman, a writer maybe, was sitting in a corner reading to a group of small children. They were laughing.

'Hurry up,' said Sylvie. 'Pick something. Anything.'

Usually Holly spent a long time looking at the books trying to decide what to chose. Today she pulled three quickly off the shelf without even taking time to read the blurbs.

As she turned to go back to the desk she bumped into Anna.

'Oh, hi there, Holly.'

'Hi,' mumbled Holly, who had been hoping to slide out of the door without seeing anyone she knew.

Anna let her go in front of her in the queue, and then followed her out.

'Heading home?'

'No,' said Holly, 'I'm going up the way.' She pointed towards the centre of town.

'So am I. I want to do a bit of shopping up town. I've left Cindy in the flat. I can't take her into shops.' Anna fell into step beside Holly.

Holly looked around, trying to work out how to lose

Anna before she met up with Mum. After they'd gone a short distance she pulled up short and said, 'I'm just going in here to get something. See you!' With that she wheeled off to the right and into the nearest shop.

'See you later,' Anna called after her, obviously mystified by Holly's swift exit. From the doorway of the shop, Holly watched her walking on, heading up the hill. She breathed a sigh of relief.

The shop sold odds and ends but on the counter stood a rack of sweets and chocolate. Holly bought a bar of something – she didn't even notice what. By the time she was back out in the street there was no sign of Anna.

Holly looked at her watch. Five to eleven. She quickened her step.

She saw her mum up ahead, coming down the hill towards her. She was waving. Not long now until this ordeal was over. Holly waved back. They were only a few paces apart now.

And at that very moment, just as they were about to meet, a familiar car came swerving into the kerb and pulled up sharply with a squeal of tyres.

Twenty-one

Dad jumped out of the car, his face white and tense. He looked from Holly to Sharon and back again.

'What's going on with you two?'

'Nothing, Joe,' said Sharon quickly. 'Just thought I'd pop through to Edinburgh and see Holly for a wee while.'

Dad looked back at Holly. She felt he could see right through her. She said nothing. She couldn't think up any more lies. The bag suddenly felt far too heavy. She dropped it on the pavement.

'Watch!' cried Sharon, putting out a hand to lift it.

But Holly's dad was faster. He got to it first.

'What's in here then, Holly?' He held it up in front of her face.

'Library books,' she said dully.

'She's just been to the library, Joe,' said Sharon. 'She's done nothing wrong. Lay off her!'

'Get in the car,' he said to Holly, opening the back door. 'We're going home. You'd better come too, Sharon. There's something going on between the two of you and I want to know what it is.'

He put the bag on the front seat beside him. Sharon clambered into the back with Holly, and covered Holly's hand with hers. They drove in silence the short distance down the street.

Holly's dad carried the bag up the stairs. She and her mum walked behind. On the top landing, while Dad waited for the joiner to move aside, Sharon nudged Holly and put her finger to her lips.

Mrs McGinty was at the top of the stairs this time. She must have been watching the joiner at work. He was almost finished.

'Don't tell me you've come to live here now,' said Mrs McGinty to Sharon. 'You're never away from the place.'

'Mind your own business,' said Dad, unusually roughly for him. Holly could see that he was in no mood to put up with Mrs McGinty but she was surprised at the sharpness in his voice.

'No need to be rude,' snipped Mrs McGinty. 'I saved your house from getting burgled and what thanks do I get for it? If it hadn't been for me –'

Holly's dad led the way into the flat. He was keeping a firm grip on the bag.

'I'll just be another couple of minutes,' said the joiner.

'Fine,' said Holly's dad.

They went into the kitchen.

'Will I put the kettle on?' asked Holly and without waiting for a reply, she turned on the tap, spraying water over the draining board. She had never felt this nervous before. It was as if a clap of thunder was about to break over their heads.

'A cuppa would be great, pet,' said Sharon. She too sounded nervous. 'I'm fair parched.'

Dad left them to go and have a final word with the joiner. He took the bag with him.

'Just say you don't know how the packet got in there or anything about it,' whispered Sharon quickly.

Holly stared at her. Did she really think they could get away with it? With Dad on the war path? The kettle boiled and she filled up the teapot.

They heard the front door close. That must be the joiner leaving.

Dad came back to join them. Holly poured the tea.

'Now then, what's this all about, Holly?' he asked. His voice wasn't so angry now, but she could tell that he was upset.

She stared into her cup.

'OK, then, let's see what's in here.' He took the three library books from the bag and laid them on the table. Then he lifted out the package wrapped in the plastic bag and held it up.

He looked first at Holly and then at Sharon. Neither said anything. He put his hand into the plastic bag and took out the package. He turned it over several times, examining it.

'What's this?'

'Dunno,' said Holly. It was true. She didn't actually know, did she? She had simply *guessed* that it might be drugs.

Dad raised his eyebrows. He didn't believe her. 'What have you been up to, Holly?' And Holly realised then what she had known all along. She should have told Dad right away.

'It's not her fault, Joe,' Sharon spilled out. 'It was all a mistake. You see, Lenny got this call –'

'Oh yes, Lenny!' Dad gave a harsh laugh. 'So he's involved in this, is he? I might have known. Better come clean, Sharon.'

Holly closed her eyes while Sharon told Dad the story of the package, of how it had fallen out of her bag and how Holly had picked it up and kept it by mistake, and why she needed it back so urgently.

Dad pushed the package into the middle of the table. 'You should never have let Holly go anywhere near your flat! What have you got her into?'

'Joe, I had no idea that Holly had picked up the package in the station,' stressed Sharon, her eyes huge with tears. 'It was while you were talking to me that she did it. I had my back to her.'

'So it's my fault, is it?' Dad retorted. 'What were you doing carrying drugs around in your bag to start with?' he demanded.

'I've never done it before.'

'How am I supposed to believe that? You're a fool, Sharon!'

'Dad,' protested Holly. She was near tears now.

'Holly, I'll ask you to stay out of this – as you should have done from the start. Your mum's put you in real danger.' He turned back to Sharon. 'I am right, am I? There are illegal drugs in there, Sharon?'

Mum nodded. 'I couldn't help it, Joe. Lenny made me take it.'

'*Made* you?'

'He'd have been in trouble if the police had come and found it in the flat.'

'So what! The sooner that man is locked up the better it'll be for you. For *all* of us.'

'Lenny's not that bad. He's not violent or anything. It's just that his friend –'

'His friend made him do it? Did he?'

Mum's voice was low as she grabbed Holly's hand. 'You don't know these people, Joe. You don't understand.'

'What I don't understand is how you could involve your daughter – *our* daughter – in something like this.'

'I didn't mean to, Joe.'

Holly's dad silenced Sharon with a look. 'One word to the Social Services about this . . .'

Mum held up a hand, pleading. 'I am going to get out of it, Joe. Honest. I've finished with Lenny.'

Dad sat back down in his chair and took a deep breath. 'I'd like to believe that, I really would.'

'I swear, Joe. I don't want to get myself in trouble with the police.' There was a pause. 'Or Holly.'

'I don't know what you want, Sharon.' Dad put his hand to his forehead and closed his eyes for a moment.

The package lay on the table in front of them and Dad lifted his head to stare at it. So did Holly. And Sharon. It looked so harmless. Just a plain sealed packet. But it might as well have been a ticking time bomb as far as the three of them were concerned.

'Joe?' asked Sharon after a few moments. 'What can we do?'

There was a pause before Dad replied. 'Hand it over to the police,' he said quietly.

'No, you can't!' Mum began to cry. 'What'll I tell –'

'What'll you tell who? Lenny? And there was me thinking you and Lenny had broken up, for good.'

'We have, Joe. I promise. But there's Jacko. And there are others. They'll ask questions,' said Sharon. 'Lots of questions.'

Dad glanced at Sharon. There was real fear in her voice.

'The police'll ask questions too,' he said quietly. 'These men should be stopped.'

But Holly could tell that he wasn't sure. Her dad was an honest man, Holly knew that. He obeyed all the rules. He didn't drop litter, drink and drive, or tell lies, and if he was given too much change in a shop he would always go back and return it. He knew what he should do, but Holly could tell that he didn't want Mum to be in any more trouble than she was.

'I'm in an impossible situation,' he said. 'You've put me in an impossible situation, Sharon.'

Twenty-two

The silence in the room was deafening. Holly realised she was holding her breath, waiting for her father to make his decision. Sharon's eyes were glued to his face.

'I don't want to shop you, Sharon,' said Dad finally.

Holly let out her breath.

'Oh, Joe! That's so good of you, Joe,' said Sharon, reaching for his hand. 'Thank you! I knew you wouldn't.'

'You are Holly's mother after all.' He pulled his hand away. 'But you need to start acting like it. Can't you see how this is affecting her?'

'I know you think I'm a rubbish mother but I love her.' Sharon put her hand over Holly's instead. 'More than anything.'

Holly blinked to keep the tears back.

'I'll take this back to Lenny and . . .' Sharon's free hand crept across the table to the package.

'Sharon! In the name . . . !' Dad shook his head in astonishment and slammed his hand over the package. 'Why would you want to do that?

'But, Joe –'

'I'm not going to play any part in helping your friend Lenny to put drugs out there. Some kids will end up with them. Kids like Holly.'

Holly met her dad's frustrated gaze. It was as if he

thought he was the only one there that understood.

'For goodness sake, Sharon. Think! Drugs are dangerous. You must realise that.'

But Sharon shrugged. 'They'd just get hold of them somewhere else.'

'Not with my help, at any rate.' Dad glared at her.

'But what am I going to do about Lenny and Billy? And Jacko? He's a horror. You don't know what it's like. They'll all be after me. That lot there's worth a bomb.'

For one crazy moment Holly wanted to ask her dad to let her mum stay here, safe with them. But the idea only lasted for a moment. Mum would be grateful and all would be fine for a couple of days, but then she'd get restless and she'd leave just as she had three or four years back. Dad couldn't forgive her for that.

'What am I going to do?' asked Sharon, tearful again.

Holly's dad turned to face her. Did he expect *Holly* to find an answer?

'He expects you to do the right thing,' said Sylvie. All through this horrible series of events Holly had been trying to stop her mum from getting into trouble, but was that really the right thing to do? Holly remembered the words Dad had said to her after the stramash at Cerise's house: *I know my girl knows better than that.*

'You could take that package to the police yourself,' Holly said quietly, looking at her mum. 'You could tell them the whole story, including the bit about Lenny breaking into our flat . . .'

'Put the blame on Lenny, where it belongs,' added Dad, giving Holly a look of such pride that she couldn't help but smile. 'Let him carry the can, and then you get out and stay out, stay clear of the whole lot of them. They are a bad lot. Get a new phone, change your phone number, move into a different flat, get a new job. Maybe even move to a new city. It's hard, but if you really want out, Sharon, you have to make changes.'

Sharon bit her lip and in a very small voice said, 'But Lenny knows that Holly picked up the bag.'

Anger flared again in Holly's dad. 'Because you told him, presumably?'

Sharon didn't answer.

'How stupid can you *be*?'

Sharon shrugged and shook her head. She looked beaten.

'There's no point in me going on about it any more now. What's done is done. Holly's told you what you need to do.'

'But what'll I say to him?' Sharon's voice wavered. 'To Lenny?'

'You say nothing to him. Nothing. Go back to Glasgow, go to the police, hand over the package, answer their questions as honestly as you can and stay out of Lenny's way,' said Dad. 'You don't need to say another word to that man. Ever.'

'You make it sound so easy.' Sharon was staring at the package.

Dad pushed it slowly towards her end of the table. 'It's not easy, I know, Sharon, but it's what needs to be done. And Holly needs to know that you can do that – *we* need to know you've put an end to it. Can you honestly expect me to let you see Holly on your own unless I am sure that she's not going to be exposed to drug dealers like Lenny? You're lucky I'm not taking you and that package straight to the nearest police station and turning you in. You've got the chance to do the right thing.'

Sharon nodded slowly. 'So, I'll take the package, and take it the police station and explain about it.' It was as if she was trying to memorise the instructions.

'The whole story,' said Dad, nodding.

'But they'll check it for fingerprints,' said Sharon suddenly, her eyes wide with fear. 'Mine, Holly's and yours!'

'I've no doubt the police will be in touch,' said Dad grimly.

Sharon got to her feet, holding onto the table edge to steady herself. She wrapped the package up in the plastic bag again and pushed it to the bottom of her carrier.

'Will you be all right, Mum?' Holly stood up and put her arm round her shoulders.

'I'll be fine, love. Don't you worry yourself about me.'

'Do you see what you're putting your daughter through?' Dad was still upset.

'I didn't mean –' said Sharon.

'Not again!' he exclaimed. 'Just do the right thing. For her sake, if not your own.' He simmered down and then picked up his car keys. 'I'll run you to the station,' he said wearily.

'That'd be great, Joe.'

Holly went with them. She sat in the back and held her mum's hand. Sharon kept telling her not worry.

Dad drove down the slope into the station and pulled up to let Sharon out.

'Can't wait for long,' he warned. 'I've got two taxis on my tail.'

Sharon gave Holly a hug and a kiss and said again, 'I'll be OK. I'll see you soon, love. Thanks for the lift, Joe. Sorry again for all the bother. And I'll take your advice. I'll go to the police. I will.'

Holly watched her mum as she walked through the crowds, carrying the bag containing the package. At the corner Sharon turned and waved quickly, before heading off for the Glasgow train.

'She'll survive,' sighed Holly's dad as he started up the engine. 'She always seems to, somehow or other.'

Holly hoped he was right. Sharon was moving deeper into the crowd now, her head bobbing along amongst all the other passengers.

Twenty-three

'What's up?' asked Johnny, snapping his fingers in front of Holly's face and making her blink. 'You're miles away. You're not concentrating.'

It was raining. They were playing chess, and Holly was losing, badly. Tim and Lauren were playing Scrabble in the kitchen.

'Nothing.'

'Must be *something*. Is it about your mum?'

Holly's head jerked up. 'How d'you know?'

'Well, you've said things from time to time.'

'Have I?'

'Yeah. That you worry about her. You don't like some of her friends.'

'I don't!' Holly burst out. 'Some of them are –' She shrugged. 'Not very nice.'

'That why you don't live with her?' Johnny had never really concerned himself with the details of how Holly came to live in Edinburgh with her Dad.

'Guess so. Dad's a bit more . . . reliable.'

'Sounds like your mum can probably take care of herself.'

'Yes,' said Holly. But she wasn't absolutely confident about that.

'I'm about to take your queen,' said Johnny. He

punched the air and laughed. He loved winning. 'A walkover! Shall we start again? This time you might concentrate more.'

'I was concentrating!'

'You weren't!'

'Stop bullying me!'

'Me? Bully you? Would I do that?'

'Yes.'

Johnny grinned. 'I'd better mend my ways then. That's what Ma says. I'm just bossy, that's all. Dithery people like you need bossy people like me.'

Holly burst out laughing. 'You are so rude!'

Johnny nodded, smiling as if she had paid him an enormous compliment. He began to set up the board again. 'Anyway, how's your dad getting on with that bright pink woman?'

'Cerise?'

'That's the one.'

Holly gave a big sigh. 'It's finished. Dad told me.' He had explained the previous evening while they were clearing up after supper. He had met Cerise for a drink one day and they'd had what he called 'a very civilized conversation'. Apparently they were still friends, although Dad hadn't sounded sure that he would be seeing her again.

'Thank goodness for that then,' said Johnny. 'She sounded a bit of a nightmare. Shall we play?'

Before long, Holly got caught up in the game again and forgot about her mum and Lenny and Dad and Cerise and the rest of them, for the meantime, at least.

Holly didn't manage to speak to her mum for a while. She left some voicemail messages the first couple of days after she had gone back to Glasgow with the package, and got a couple of texts in reply saying, 'I'm fine. Don't worry. No problems.' But after that there was nothing.

Dad said he'd heard nothing from Mum either. 'We have to try and trust her, love. She's maybe changed her number like I told her. I'm sure she'll be in touch. She knows that I meant it when I said she couldn't see you unless it was all sorted out.'

But would that be enough to persuade Mum to hand the drugs over to the police? To risk angering Lenny and his mates? Holly wasn't sure. She tried hard not to think too deeply about it. There was a lot on her plate at the moment – not least worrying about her new school. A few of her friends from her primary class were going too, but not many. Would she be able to make new friends? She wished she was more like Lauren, with her easy confidence. Lauren was looking forward to going to her new school, along with Johnny and Tim. Although a few days earlier, Lauren had surprised Holly by thanking her. 'What for?' Holly was mystified. 'For hanging out with me this summer.'

'Don't be daft!' Holly blushed.

'No, really,' Lauren had looked serious. 'I'm quite nervous about this next term, so it's good knowing that I've got you as a friend out of school.' Holly had never thought about it like that. Lauren had become a good friend, despite Holly's misgivings when they were first introduced.

Then, one evening, when Holly and Dad were having a meal at Anna's – they often seemed to be invited there these days – Holly's mobile rang. It wasn't a number she recognised.

'Hi, pet. It's me.'

'Oh, hi, Mum.' A feeling of relief flooded Holly. So Dad was right – Mum had a new number!

'Can I have a wee word?'

That usually meant out of earshot of Holly's dad.

'Can I go into the hall, Dad?' asked Holly. 'It's Mum.'

He raised his eyebrows, and nodded. He looked pleased.

'Listen, love,' said Sharon, 'I'm going away for a bit.' She sounded bright and happy – it was ages since Holly had heard her like this.

'Where to?'

'Portugal. Not sure how long for, maybe a few weeks. Or months.'

'Portugal? You liked it when you went there before.'

'I know! How lucky am I!'

'Who . . . who are you going with, Mum?' Holly closed her eyes.

'Well. You mind Jerry, that guy at the cafe in the station I was speaking to? The one that knew me from the *Spike*?'

This wasn't the answer Holly had expected. 'The one cleaning the tables?'

'That was only a temporary job he had. Just while he was waiting for work. He got laid off from his job with the council. Redundancy, you know. Anyway, his brother's got a wee place in Portugal that he's not using at present so he said we can have it. . .' Holly listened as her mum got wrapped up in telling her more about her plans. 'It's got a swimming pool and everything. Jerry's going to do some painting and decorating instead of paying rent. And I might get a job in a bar.'

Holly found that she was smiling. 'I didn't know you were seeing him,' she said. 'Quick work, Mum!' she teased.

Sharon laughed. 'It's fairly recent, like. He's a nice guy, Jerry. Met him at the *Spike* a couple of weeks back, on my last night there, actually. Nothing bent about him.' Sharon's voice raised a pitch. 'Holly, I've really got to get away from here for a while. You do understand, don't you? Next time it'll be with you, like I promised. Like we planned.'

'Yes, of course. You could do with a break.' Holly knew that her mum meant what she said, but she also knew that a holiday together was unlikely. 'What's happened to Lenny, Mum?' she asked carefully.

'He got pulled in by the police. Not long after I saw you last. Him and Jacko and Billy, and there were a few others too. It was nothing to do with our stuff.'

Our stuff! Holly shuddered at the memory. 'What had he done?' she asked.

'He was caught with drugs on him.'

Holly wondered briefly whether to ask if Mum had

done as she promised and gone to the police with the package, but something told her not to. Like Dad said, they had to trust her.

'Anyway, we're off in the morning,' said Sharon quickly. 'I wanted you to know. I'm sorry I haven't seen you, but it's all been a bit last minute . . .' Her voice trailed off.

'I'm going to miss you, Mum,' gulped Holly.

'I know, pet. I'll miss you too. Maybe you could come out for a week? How would you like that?'

'You mean to Portugal?'

'Why not?'

Typical Mum. She never really thought about things the way a parent should. 'I'm starting school again soon. Next week. And anyway, Dad'd never let me.'

'Aw, that's a pity.' And Sharon really did sound as if she meant it. 'I'll keep in touch, though.'

She always did when she went away. One way or another.

'How long did you say you were going for?' asked Holly.

'Not sure right now. Depends. But I'll be back, love. I promise you I will. Bye, love!'

Holly stood in the hall once the line went dead. She saved her mum's new phone number into her contacts, and deleted the old one. She could hear the low hum of Anna chatting to her dad in the kitchen. She would wait until she and Dad were back home before telling him Mum's news.

She was glad that her mum was getting away from all

that trouble in Glasgow. She'd be safer in Portugal. And she had promised that she would be back.

'She will keep her promise,' Sylvie assured her. 'She always does come back.'

And Sylvie was usually right.

About the Author

Joan Lingard has published more than thirty books for children and thirteen for adults. *Tug of War* was shortlisted for the Carnegie Medal, the Federation of Children's Book Groups Award, the Lancashire Children's Book Club of the Year, and the Sheffield Book Award. *The Eleventh Orphan* was shortlisted for The Royal Mail Award for Scottish Children's Books. Joan was awarded an M.B.E. in 1998.

'I was an avid reader when I was young (still am!) and could never get enough to read. I used to go to my local children's library, a poor affair housed in something resembling a shed, and no bigger. The books were all ancient and had lost their dust wrappers, and the pages were often spattered with the remains of other readers' meals, but it would have taken more than that to put me off. I read very fast and when I finished a book I moaned in my mother's ear about having nothing to read. One day, fed up with me, she said, "Why don't you write a book of your own?" "Why not?" I thought. I took lined, foolscap paper, filled my fountain pen with green ink (I thought that would be artistic!), and I began to write my very first novel. From that moment on I wanted to be a novelist, and nothing else.' *Joan Lingard*

What to do about Holly

by JOAN LINGARD

*'Come on, Holly,' said her mother, grabbing her free hand.
'And stop dragging yer feet or you'll miss yer train.'*

'I'm not wantin' to go on the train on my own.'

*'Well, you'll have to, won't you? I can't take you,
I've my work to go to.'*

When Holly's mother puts her on the Edinburgh
train, in the care of a complete stranger, who happens
to be a children's author, none of them have any idea
of what is going to happen.

The following weeks will be unlike anything
Holly has known before; Nina and Colin Nightingale,
and their son Johnny live a life very different to her
own. But when Johnny has a terrible accident all
differences are forgotten.

The Eleventh Orphan
by JOAN LINGARD

Mr and Mrs Bigsby of the *Pig and Whistle*,
Stoke Newington already look after ten children.
When Constable O'Dowd bring them an
eleventh orphan he found on the streets,
Ma Bigsby is reluctant to take her.

But there's something about Elfie, it's 1900,
the first day of a new century and Ma loves
a mystery. Just why does Elfie possess a little
watercolour of the *Pig and Whistle*?

As the mystery unfolds, Elfie's world
will change completely.

Shortlisted for the Royal Mail Awards

The Chancery Lane Conspiracy
by JOAN LINGARD

It's Joe's first day in a solicitor's office in
Chancery Lane, where Elfie's father has taken him
in as a clerk. But there's a new partner in the firm
who seems to have a hold over Mr Trelawney –
and who takes an instant dislike to Joe.

Joe and Elfie are sure there's more to this
man than meets the eye and they are determined
to find out what.

Their investigations soon uncover a conspiracy
that stretches from one end of the country
to the other.

The Stolen Sister

by JOAN LINGARD

When Elfie's little sister, Rosalind Trelawney,
is stolen from outside her school, her parents will
do anything to get her back. But Rosalind's safe
return comes at great cost . . .

As Elfie and Joe untangle the threads of the
kidnappers' plot, it leads them closer to a devious
mastermind who will stop at nothing – not
even murder. It's a race against time to locate
the villain before Elfie's family falls apart
under the strain.

THE FILE ON FRAULEIN BERG
by JOAN LINGARD

1944. Belfast. The War drags on. Kate, Harriet and Sally read spy stories and imagine themselves dropping over enemy lines to perform deeds of great daring.

When Fraulein Berg, a real German, arrives at their school it doesn't take them long to work out that their new teacher is a spy. Now the girls have a mission. To watch her. Follow her. Track down her every secret. Prove she is the enemy.

But the File on Fraulein Berg reveals a very different story – one that will haunt Kate for the rest of her life.

You can find out more about other
exciting Catnip books by visiting:

www.catnippublishing.co.uk